Peter Conway lives in Somerset.

UNWILLINGLY TO SCHOOL

Janet Creswell is struggling to come to terms with her husband's sudden death when she receives a visit from Richard Medley, a former pupil at Brantwood preparatory school in Sussex, where in 1944 she'd been matron. Their meeting evokes memories. However, it also raises serious doubts regarding the headmaster, Edward Blackstone, as well as questions about the maltreatment of the boys. And his drowning in the swimming pool — had it been an accident, or murder? Her curiosity piqued, Janet meets people involved in the school at that time, and finally discovers the truth about those distant, disturbing events.

PETER CONWAY

UNWILLINGLY TO SCHOOL

Complete and Unabridged

ULVERSCROFT
Leicester

First published in Great Britain in 2007 by
Robert Hale Limited
London

First Large Print Edition
published 2008
by arrangement with
Robert Hale Limited
London

British Library CIP Data

Conway, Peter, *1929 –*
    Unwillingly to school.—Large print ed.—
    Ulverscroft large print series: crime
    1. Teachers—England—Fiction 2. Boarding schools
    —England—Fiction 3. Detective and mystery stories
    4. Large type books
    I. Title
    823.9′14 [F]

    ISBN 978–1–84782–248–2

Published by
F. A. Thorpe (Publishing)
Anstey, Leicestershire

Set by Words & Graphics Ltd.
Anstey, Leicestershire
Printed and bound in Great Britain by
T. J. International Ltd., Padstow, Cornwall

This book is printed on acid-free paper

1

It was when I was going through the contents of my mother's desk that I came across the folder in the bottom drawer. I very nearly missed it as it was under a jumble of pieces of material that she had been using to work on the patchwork quilt before her eyesight began to fail. She had so hated the loss of vision due to macular degeneration that had started two years earlier and even more the insidious deterioration in her memory that had begun at much the same time. In a sense, therefore, the fatal brain haemorrhage that had followed a fall in her kitchen was a relief to us all.

Inside the folder was a typewritten manuscript and I took it through to the living-room, armed myself with a glass and a bottle of beer and began to read.

This account is for me and no one else. I am writing it to remind myself of how I managed to pull myself out of the 'slough of despond' into which I had descended after my husband Frank's sudden death. It has also allowed me to relive the most exciting few months of my life. Janet Cresswell. December 2000.

'You'll do the trolley round at the hospital this afternoon, won't you, Janet?'

Madge Renton's booming voice over the line brooked no refusal and even if I had been my normal self, I would have been hard pressed to turn her down, much though I disliked bullies. And a bully the woman most certainly was, with her finger in every pie, ordering this and directing that. My trouble was that I wasn't my normal self and hadn't been ever since Frank's sudden death six months earlier and, despite it being the last thing I felt like doing that day, I weakly gave in.

It had been so cruel. Frank was a year or two younger than me and after we had both retired we had a wonderful time together. He was full of energy both physical and mental and he kept up his golf. We played tennis as quite a formidable mixed doubles partnership; went for long walks on the South Downs; did some sailing and enjoyed the Chichester Festival. And then, quite suddenly, it was all over. The night it happened, we had planned to watch a late night arts programme on TV, but just before it was due to start, Frank had got to his feet and it was so unlike him that I remember looking up at him with some concern.

'Are you feeling all right?'

'Of course I am, never better.'

He came across and gave me a kiss and then he was gone. I knew from my experience in medicine that the bereaved often go through an 'if only' stage, but that knowledge did nothing to protect me from it. If only the video recorder had been working and I had gone up to bed with him; if only I had taken more notice of the fact that he was looking grey and that there were beads of sweat on his forehead when he said goodnight to me; if only I had checked to see how he was before I slipped into bed beside him an hour later.

I suppose I ought to have been thankful that Frank didn't survive to be left a cardiac cripple, which he would have hated, but I wasn't. Other people survived bad heart attacks and were able to live full and active lives afterwards, so why not him?

On the face of it, I suppose that initially I must have appeared to be coping well enough, but my children and friends didn't know about the emptiness, the aching void in my life. Frank had been that life for nearly fifty years and I had no idea how I was going to carry on without him. He had been my husband, my lover, my companion, the father of my children and my partner in medicine. Husband and wife general practices may not always work, but ours did. Frank and I each had our special interests, mine being paediatrics and obstetrics and his psychiatry and skin disorders, and whenever there was a problem, there was always the other to give advice and support. We did introduce other partners when I became pregnant, but we had started the practice and it remained ours until we retired. Maybe all that sounds too good to be true and I am looking back on our marriage through rose-tinted spectacles, but I'm not. Of course we had our minor tiffs and I won't say that I didn't have my jealous moments early in our marriage. Frank liked women and that feeling was certainly reciprocated. I had talked to enough husbands in my time in our practice to know that many men, perhaps the majority, seemed unable to do without sexual variety. Had he been one of them? I didn't know; I didn't dare to ask him in case he admitted it and later on, my fears seemed both ridiculous and, more than that, no longer to matter.

After the initial shock was over and I had finished sorting out his affairs, I steadily began to sink into a state of apathy, in which anything and everything was too much trouble and it wasn't until that visit to the hospital and in particular the adolescent psychiatric unit, that I received the sudden sharp shock that was needed to help me snap out of it. I am neither an emotional nor a quick-tempered person, but the sight of the 15-year-old girl to whom I sold a bottle of shampoo and who was obviously suffering from advanced anorexia nervosa, produced in me a sudden feeling of revulsion and anger deep inside me. In my time as a GP, I had perhaps had three cases in my practice. I had seen pictures in the medical journals, but never before had I come face to face with a walking skeleton wearing nothing but a thin nightdress and weighing little more than five stone. How could she be doing such a thing to herself?

Almost at once, though, I realized how unreasonable my immediate reaction had been. Who was I to be blaming a young girl for a condition about which I knew precious little and about whose background I knew nothing, when I, too, had lost weight, had withdrawn from almost all my previous activities and was feeling pathetically sorry for myself? Hadn't I had robust health, nearly fifty years of happy married life and two children who were both successful in their different ways? I hadn't even had the good sense to admit either to my GP or my children that I was miserable, lonely and saw no future for myself. Instead, I tried and to some extent succeeded in hiding it from them. Why hadn't Paul, my son, who was doing so well as a successful chest physician in London, not noticed and done something about it? The answer was that like Frank and, to an even greater extent my father, he was an outgoing, ebullient person, who had little patience with people who were unable to cope with life's vicissitudes.

Looking back, I think I had always had a subconscious fear that I might turn out to be like my mother and I compensated for it by being an over-confident adolescent and young adult. She, poor woman, had clearly suffered from a severe and intractable post-natal depression and had been a remote and shadowy figure to me right up until the time she had died when I was fifteen and away at boarding-school. My father told me that it had been the result of a long-standing illness. At the time it hadn't occurred to me that she might have committed suicide and when I did wonder about that at medical school, I hadn't either the heart or the inclination to tackle him about it.

He could hardly have been a more different person from my mother. He was a cheerful, jolly man, full of energy and very good at games. He was also a very tactile individual, the one who used to kiss and hug me when I was a small girl, who held my hand when we went for walks and who read me stories when I used to snuggle up to him after tea in front of the fire on cold winter afternoons and when I was in bed before he switched out the light. It was he who taught me to ride a bicycle and to play both table and lawn tennis to quite a high standard. We also went to cricket matches together at Hove to watch Sussex and he rigged up a net in the garden, where we would bowl at each other for hours.

Was he trying to turn me into the son he wished he had had? I don't think so. He handled my adolescence both directly and tactfully and was open and unembarrassed about sex instruction. He didn't confine himself to the simple facts, either; sex, he told me, had been used as a weapon for centuries, by secular and religious leaders and thinkers as an instrument of control and by men to keep women in their place. No wonder that women in the previous century had been so ignorant and found it so distasteful when they had been brought up to believe that it was a duty and an ordeal that had to be suffered so that children could be born. It was hardly surprising, either, that men should have found it boring and unfulfilling with their wives and that prostitution should have thrived. Sex shouldn't be like that at all, he went on. It should be the joyful expression of people's love for one another, it should be fun and one should use one's imagination to make it more so. Many men in his position in those inter-war years would have tried to turn an only daughter into a housekeeper, but not him. He encouraged me to take up a career and never to believe that women were second-class citizens.

Following my visit to the hospital for that trolley round, I started to take trouble over my personal appearance again. I arranged for a firm of contract cleaners to sort out the house, which I had been sadly neglecting, and then managed to get hold of a cheerful, young single mother with a baby to come on a weekly basis to keep it in order. I even managed to restart some social activities, joining a spirited, albeit geriatric, group of players at my tennis club.

It was some three months later when I was having breakfast that I heard the arrival of the postman and went through into the hall. There was just one envelope on the carpet under the letter-box and when I lifted it up I noticed the London postmark and the unfamiliar handwriting. I took it through to the kitchen, slit it open and read it over my second cup of coffee.

Dear Mrs Cresswell
I don't suppose you remember me; I was one of the boys at Brantwood when you were there in 1944. I happened to be passing the school, which is now a health farm, the other day and all the memories came flooding back. I would very much like to have a chat about those old times and was wondering if I might look in to see you. I have recently retired and my time is my own.
Yours sincerely
Richard Medley.

When I had finished the letter, I sat back in my favourite armchair and closed my eyes. How that letter took me back! I had been born and brought up in Chichester and the decision to move back there when Frank and I retired had not been a difficult one; we both loved the area and it was within easy reach of our children. My father had been one of the local GPs and when, in 1944, I had a year to fill in between getting my higher certificate and first MB and starting at the Royal Free Hospital Medical School, he heard that there was a job available as under-matron at

Brantwood, a preparatory school for boys near Midhurst. He knew old Dr Franklin, the school doctor, who had been dredged up from retirement earlier in the war, and that was how the contact had been made.

Nowadays, girls of the age I was then, like my granddaughter, go off to Australia, or do voluntary service in Africa, but when I was eighteen, the war was still on and opportunities like that didn't exist. Brantwood! The school's very name had the same effect on me as it had obviously had on Richard Medley and immediately I began to recall incidents that up to that moment had been buried deeply in my subconscious. The Freudians wouldn't like me for saying it, but I think it was an example of good, healthy repression. I was, after all, at that time still a young girl — people didn't mature so quickly in those days as they do now — exciting times were ahead of me and my subconscious in its wisdom had no doubt decided that for an 18-year-old the present and the future were quite enough for me to cope with, without having to dwell on the uncomfortable things that had happened there.

The printing on the letterhead rather grandly stated that it was from Professor Richard Medley, FRS, and as soon as it opened at 9.30, I walked round to the public library and looked him up in *Who's Who*. A double first at Cambridge, medical school at the Middlesex Hospital, a return to academic life with a Fellowship at King's College, Cambridge and finally the Chair of Physiology at University College, London, was no mean career. His entry was quite short and there were few personal details. He appeared to be unmarried, lived in London and his interests were listed as chess, stamp collecting and opera.

I couldn't help smiling to myself at the thought that such a miserable small boy should have made such a name for himself. I remembered him now quite vividly; he had been of more than average height for his age, but weedy, hopelessly uncoordinated and myopic. When one combined those physical liabilities with the fact that he was one of the two brightest boys in the school, there existed the classical recipe for bullying and he had certainly been the victim of that. I couldn't recall his name, but there had been one overgrown oaf in the same dormitory who used to make his life a particular misery. What I completely failed to understand was why Richard Medley wanted to chat to me of all people, who, after all, had only been at Brantwood for one term, about the school more than fifty years after he had left. How

11

had he traced me? I also found it difficult to believe that 'just passing the school', would have been sufficient motivation for him to take so much trouble.

It was not until I found myself whistling as I was doing some housework that I realized to my great surprise that I felt more alive and cheerful than I had since Frank's death. I had actually been thinking about something completely different from the empty future, which is what had come to occupy my mind to the exclusion of almost everything else. More and more detail about Edward Blackstone, the extraordinary headmaster of Brantwood School, was coming back to me. There and then, I switched off the vacuum cleaner and went to my desk.

Dear Richard
I hope you don't mind my calling you that — I always used to and Professor Medley sounds so formal. Of course I remember you and would love to meet you again. If it's not too far for you to come, how about lunch here one day next week? Give me a ring any morning between eight and nine and we can fix a firm date and time.
Best wishes
Yours Janet.

The man certainly didn't hang about after receiving my letter, telephoning me while I was having breakfast only two days later, and we settled for lunch the following Tuesday.

I had plenty of time in which to observe Richard Medley when he arrived. I was putting a comb through my hair in the bedroom some twenty minutes before I had expected him when an elderly Ford Fiesta appeared and was parked on the opposite side of the street. I say parked, but that was hardly an accurate statement of what occurred. Although there was perfectly adequate space available, after violent revvings, kangaroo hops and stalling three times, the car still finished a good three feet from the edge of the pavement. Medley, and I had no doubt that it was him, was a very tall man, at least six feet three, very thin, with ill-fitting clothes, bespectacled and with wispy sandy-coloured hair. After he had uncoiled himself from the interior of the car, he looked at its position, clearly decided that he wasn't going to be able to do any better and after one glance up at my house, began to stroll up the road, a leather briefcase in his hand.

There is a very accurate clock in my kitchen with a quartz movement and when I had put the potatoes on, I stood looking at it.

Much to my amusement, the doorbell rang just as the second hand clicked round to precisely 12.30. When I went to answer it, the man looked so anxious standing there that it quite removed any nervousness on my part.

'Richard? Do come in,' I said, taking hold of his hand when he showed no signs of moving. 'It is good to see you after all these years; I've often wondered what happened to you.' That was hardly the truth, but the little white lie seemed to put him a bit more at his ease.

'How did you manage to find me?' I asked, when we had gone through into the sitting-room and I had given him some apple juice — he refused anything alcoholic.

'It wasn't all that difficult,' he replied. 'In fact, I struck oil at the first attempt. You see, I remembered that you were going to medical school and The Royal Free seemed the most likely choice for a woman in the 1940s. They had your married name and even your address in their records, so one phone call was all that was necessary.'

We chatted in a rather desultory fashion over lunch; I explained about my roots in Chichester and just dropped into the conversation that I had been in practice with my husband in Wimbledon before our retirement and that I had been widowed some time. He told me something about his career as a scientist and that he was now living alone in London also in retirement. After we had finished our coffee, though, he suddenly seemed to make up his mind.

'You're no doubt wondering why I've avoided bringing up the subject of Brantwood.' I nodded. 'The answer is that I wasn't being truthful when I wrote to you to say that I just happened to be passing the school — I went down there quite deliberately. I also implied just now that my life had been rewarding and a success. Well, in a material and, to some extent, an academic sense, I suppose it has, but emotionally and in other ways, it has been a complete and utter disaster. I think that in large measure Brantwood was responsible for that, which is why I went down there. Why should it be that I've only just come to that conclusion? It's not going to be easy, but let me try to explain. You see . . . '

★ ★ ★

Had I made a mistake? The first day I didn't think so; by the first weekend I wasn't so sure; by the end of the first month, I was and knew that I had. Initial relief that I no longer had to teach the students the same old stuff had turned into the realization that I missed them and what had seemed the administrative grind in the college and university committees, I now looked back on with a feeling akin to nostalgia. The truth of the matter was that I was already both bored and lonely. If I didn't much like myself, I thought, then it was hardly surprising that that opinion should have been shared by everyone else and that there wasn't a single person I could describe as a close friend. It hadn't mattered when the days were busy and I was constantly in contact with people in the lab, in the canteen and at meetings, but it certainly did so now.

Why, then, had I done it, when instead of leaving at 65, I could have gone on for another two years and probably been offered laboratory facilities afterwards, secure in my position as emeritus professor and former head of one of the most prestigious physiological departments in the country? It had all started with a stupid row about space, which had turned into a confrontation with Craxton, the Professor of Anatomy. I had threatened to resign; my bluff had been called and not only had I been too stubborn to back down, but I had also to face the truth that I had virtually no supporters and my departure was viewed by the others, even those in my own department, with at best equanimity and at worst relief.

I had tried to tell myself that the whole thing was a blessing in disguise and that by retiring that bit early I would still be young enough to travel and pursue interests outside my work that I had never had time to develop. Once again, the truth wasn't exactly reassuring; I had had all the travel I ever wanted over the years on the conference circuit and work had been so all-pervasive in my life that I had precious few outside interests and no serious hobbies at all.

I put it off for a couple of years and then what did I do? I went down to Ringwood to pour out my woes to my mother. Put like that, even to myself it sounded pathetic; a 67-year-old professor, an FRS no less, going to cry on Mummy's shoulder, not when the going had got really rough, but merely when I found that I couldn't cope with a pathetic little crisis in my life.

It wasn't like that, though. Over the years, my mother was the one person who had really counted; she had always been there to encourage me when I was feeling insecure, to appreciate my academic achievements and to comfort me whenever I felt low.

Life couldn't have been much fun for her

after she had been widowed in her late twenties, I thought, particularly with a puny small boy to look after, but I had never heard her complain or bewail her fate and she had never become possessive in later life when she had had every excuse to do so. I only had very shadowy memories of my father, who had been killed at Dunkirk when I was only eight, but from what my mother had said and from the look of the man in military uniform in the silver-framed photograph which she kept on the piano, I had an instinct that he, who by all accounts had been a tough, games-playing extrovert, wouldn't have approved of what his son had been as a small boy, or what he was to become later. I didn't suppose that the word wimp had been invented in the forties, but it described me, as I was then, to perfection.

That first evening at my mother's, I was just about to launch into a catalogue of my miseries and misfortunes, when she put all such thoughts, at least temporarily, out of my mind.

'I'm so glad you've come down to stay, Richard dear,' she said, 'because I've decided that the time has come for me to go into sheltered accommodation. I wanted to tell you about it face to face — a letter's so impersonal, don't you think?'

I was so taken aback that all I could do was stare at her.

'But . . . ' I began feebly.

'I've thought it all out. I'm not far off ninety, as you well know; this house is far too big for me and the stairs are already a struggle. I've found ever such a nice place in Bournemouth where I can have my own room and look after myself for as long as I am able and after that there's help and even a nursing wing when things get too difficult. I know that you must be thinking that it's very expensive, but I've gone into all that, too, and with the sale of this house, I'll be able to manage very nicely without being a drain on you.'

Apart from realizing immediately that what she was saying would be right for her, I also knew her well enough to be quite certain that what she needed at that moment was reassurance and support, not objections.

'I think that's an eminently sensible and courageous decision,' I said, going over to her and giving her a hug.

'I just knew you'd understand, dear. It will be a wrench having to give up the garden, but Mr Taylor's been wanting to retire for a year or two. He's only kept on coming here because he's been with me so long and it's not even as if I've been able to give him much of a hand recently.'

'Has the place you're going to go to got a nice garden?'

'A really lovely one — that's one of the reasons why I know I'll be at home there.'

'As always, you seem to have everything beautifully organized, but there must be something I can do to help.'

'Yes, dear, there is. There's a trunk in the loft full of old photographs and other bits and pieces and you could help me to sort them out. It'll be nice to see them again and I expect you'd like to keep some of the ones I don't want.'

The trunk proved to be a veritable treasure chest. After we'd been through the contents and my mother had selected a couple of albums that she wanted to keep with her when she moved, I decided to take the remainder, together with a few other things, back to London to go through them at my leisure. I began the task that same evening, beginning with pictures of my parents and grandparents, but I knew perfectly well that the only reason for doing so was to put off facing up to the memories provoked by the series of books in which my mother had lovingly charted my life. I had had absolutely no idea that she had been doing it, but there it all was, from a record of my birth weight right up to my election to the Fellowship of the Royal Society. Every single detail was there backed by photographs, programmes of shows I had been taken to, school reports, press cuttings and reprints of all my publications, which I had sent to her more out of a sense of duty than of any feeling that she might genuinely be interested.

I was flicking through one of the middle volumes when my eye suddenly caught sight of the large photograph of the pupils and staff of Brantwood School, which occupied the whole of one page. It had been taken at the beginning of the winter term of 1944, when it had all happened, and there, sitting in the very centre of the row of chairs was my tormentor, Edward Blackstone. The mere sight of the man brought on a feeling of tight constriction in my chest that went right up into my neck, such that I was forced to sit back quietly to give it time to wear off. The man didn't look at all threatening in his well-cut sports jacket and slacks as he smiled confidently at the camera, his bald head shining in the September sunshine, but I knew differently. Immediately to Blackstone's right was Colin Hannam, the senior master and deputy head, who taught us mathematics and science, and Tony Jarrett, a young man not long down from Cambridge, who was responsible for English and History and who was unfit for military service because of his asthma. To his left was another young man and presumably he must also have been exempt from the forces for some reason or other, perhaps his sight, as he wore thick-lensed glasses. David White was dark-complexioned, with a shock of black curly hair. Looking back, I didn't think I had ever seen the man smile. He had taught us French and always seemed withdrawn and preoccupied. There were two other adults there: Barbara, the headmaster's wife, who taught piano, and supervised the housekeeping, and Janet Brice, a strikingly pretty young woman, who had just come to work as under-matron. Although I hadn't realized it at the time, looking at her picture now, I saw that she couldn't have been more than seventeen or eighteen years old at the very most.

Although I didn't remember having done so, I must at some stage have given the photograph to my mother, because in my obsessional way I had written the names of all the boys and the staff neatly in ink around the margin. Fraser, one of the world's bullies, stuck out like a sore thumb, being twice the size of anyone else. As for myself, I was conspicuous on account of my glasses — I was one of the only two boys to be wearing them — my height, my puny physique and my sticking-out ears. I was standing in the first row directly behind Mrs Blackstone and immediately to my left was Patricia, the headmaster's 12-year-old daughter. She was dressed in exactly the same way as the rest of us in grey flannel shirt and shorts, school sweater and tie. With long socks and her very short hair, she could easily have been a boy, which, looking back on it, I thought, must have been Blackstone's view of her himself.

I put the book down on the occasional table beside me and sat back in my chair, closing my eyes and remembering the misery of having to return to school at the end of the summer holidays of 1944.

2

'Can't I go to a school nearer home and as a day-boy? Please, Mum.'

'But I thought you were happy at Brantwood, dear, and you got such a good report last year, particularly from Mr Hannam. He thinks you have an excellent chance of a scholarship to Cheltenham and you know how proud that would have made your father.'

I was fed up with hearing about my father. He had been the best cricketer Brantwood had ever produced, had gone on to captain Cheltenham, had gained a blue at Cambridge and had also appeared for Hampshire on a number of occasions. That wasn't all; he had also been head boy of Brantwood, had won all the prizes and . . . the list seemed endless.

'But Mr Blackstone doesn't like me and he beats boys.'

'I'm quite sure he doesn't beat anyone who doesn't deserve it and he's never done it to you, now, has he?'

'No, but . . . '

'There you are. Anyway, he assured me when you first went there that he only ever uses the cane for very serious offences like bullying and cheating. Therefore you've absolutely nothing to worry about. You used to like Mr Blackstone when you first went to Brantwood — you were always telling me what a good sort he was. Is there anything else worrying you?'

She gave me a hug and, as always seemed to happen when someone, usually my mother, was kind and sympathetic to me, I burst into tears. I knew that she assumed that I was missing my father and that she was somehow failing me, but neither of those things was true. What made it so difficult to explain was that Blackstone had changed. When I first went to the school not long before the outbreak of the war, the man was eccentric in some ways, but he was fun and not in the least frightening; now he was terrifying. It had all come to a head the previous summer term, when Blackstone had tried to force me to eat sago pudding. I just couldn't get it down, the very sight of those fish eyes producing wave after wave of nausea, and the headmaster knew it just as well as I did. Why had the man suddenly confronted me on that occasion when I had always been excused the nauseating stuff before? God alone knew.

'Medley,' Blackstone had said, looking at

me from his position at the head of the long table, 'there is still a war on, even if at long last it looks as if we are going to win. There are going to be shortages for a very long time and faddishness is something you are going to have to overcome, most certainly before you go to public school. Mrs Stacey will give you a small helping and you will finish it up.'

I tried, I really did. I tried to imagine that it was my favourite treacle tart sitting on the plate, I shut my eyes to blot out the sight of it, I even held my nose to hide the smell, but none of it was any good. As soon as the spoon touched my lips, I began to retch and had to put it down.

'I will spare the rest of you this unseemly spectacle,' Blackstone said to the other boys, when I had finally got control of myself, 'and you may all leave, but you and I, Master Medley, will stay here until you have overcome this lamentable weakness.'

I can't remember how long I remained sitting at the table, but it must have been for all of two hours. During that time, Blackstone sat opposite me correcting a pile of exercise books and every so often looking up at me with a sinister half smile on his face. The man was playing with me and sooner or later he was going to send me up to his study and . . . If he were to cane me, I would die, I just knew it. Only two weeks earlier, the headmaster had given it to Fraser, the biggest and one of the toughest boys in the school and he had come out of the study blubbering after only three strokes.

'Medley!'

I stared across the table at the headmaster, hypnotized by those cruel, brilliant blue eyes.

'Yes, sir,' I replied, my mouth so dry that all that came out was a feeble croak.

'I have just been looking at your Latin unseen and, as you have completed the task without a single error, I suppose you can't be all bad. Run along now, otherwise you'll be late for your piano lesson.'

I hadn't really believed that I was free, not until I had run down the corridor and into the music room, where I sat down in front of the piano and began to shiver uncontrollably.

'What's the matter, Medley?'

I turned to see the headmaster's wife looking at me from the doorway.

'Nothing, Mrs Blackstone.'

'You look absolutely terrible. You'd better come up to the sickbay with me right away.'

I quite liked Mrs Blackstone. She almost never smiled and seemed remote and detached, but she was always patient with my efforts at the piano, never getting cross when I made mistake. She tried to encourage me to persist when I became discouraged, by playing the pieces to me herself and by bringing along her portable gramophone and giving me an insight into the skills of some of the great soloists of the day.

'Although you practise conscientiously and hard,' she said to me one day, 'you'll have to accept that you'll never be a really good pianist, but then I know that I'll never become a great one, which has been my most cherished ambition since I was your age, and that hasn't stopped me from getting a tremendous amount of pleasure and comfort out of it. I can tell that you already appreciate great music and being able to play the piano even averagely competently will enable you to enjoy it that much more.'

That remark had stuck in my mind because not only was it one of the few occasions that she had spoken to me at any length, but in later years I was to recognize the truth of what she had said. Had it not been for her, I would never have gone on with the piano and I knew that I would have regretted that deeply.

Despite Blackstone's unexpected action in the summer in letting me off having to eat the sago pudding, I knew that nothing had changed as soon as I arrived at Brantwood for the beginning of the winter term.

'Ah, Medley,' the man said, as he caught sight of me amongst the group of boys who had arrived by the same train, 'looking forward to the football season, are you?'

I hated football, which the head knew every bit as well as I did, and when I looked round and saw Fraser grinning at me, I thought it would have been just as inappropriate if Blackstone had asked that bullying oaf if he was looking forward to translating Latin verse.

'You look peaky, Medley, distinctly pallid. We'll have to see if we can put some colour into your cheeks in the gym, won't we?'

Physical training, or PT, as it was called then, was another thing I hated. Others could swarm up ropes without any effort at all, whereas my puny arms didn't have the strength to pull me up, and as for the horse ... How I loathed the wretched thing! Practically all the others seemed to sail over it and actually enjoy the experience — Patricia Blackstone could even do an effortless handstand and somersault over it — whereas I always landed on top of it with a sickening crash, scraping and bruising the insides of my thighs. My worst fears were realized not long after the beginning of term.

'If you don't make more effort and get over the horse next week,' Blackstone said to me at

29

the end of the PT period, 'I think we may have to see if a visit to my study will put more spring into your legs.'

The man gave me a vulpine grin and I just stood there long after he had gone, shivering and feeling sick and faint.

'You can do it, Medley, I know you can. It's rather like riding a bike — do it once and then you'll whiz over it every time. I couldn't manage it either to start with.'

I didn't believe that; Patricia was like a rubber ball and her sturdy arms and legs had real muscles, not like my feeble matchsticks. She was the same age as me and although quite a bit shorter, was a lot heavier. She positively glowed with health and vitality and although her hair, which was cut almost as short as that of the GI's we used to see walking through the town, was very fair, she had quite dark skin, which was tanned to an even coffee colour.

'Cheer up. I tell you what, there isn't time now, but I'll show you how to do it on Sunday afternoon, if you like.'

Apart from Pedlow, who was as bad at games and PT as I was, Patricia was the only friend I had at the school. Looking back on it now, it seems bizarre in the extreme. Why was it that a weed and a swot, which is what I was, and a tomboy, who was easily the best games player and, despite being a girl, the toughest person in the school, which is what she was, were almost inseparable? With the other boys, I had all the intellectual arrogance of one who found the school work childishly simple and yet with her I was endlessly patient and discovered that I had a talent for explaining things, particularly mathematics, the subject which she found the most difficult. On her side, she was fiercely protective of me. Only the previous week, Fraser had taken careful aim with his elastic band catapult, hitting me hard on the tender skin of the inner side of my thigh with a tightly folded cigarette card and made me cry.

'Wizard prang!'

'Leave him alone, Fraser.'

'Who says?'

'I do.'

Fraser was already thirteen, the biggest and tallest boy in the school and towered six inches above her.

'Oh, you do, do you?'

He gripped her by the shoulders and when he began to dig his fingers in cruelly, I saw the muscles of her neck tense. It all happened so quickly that I didn't see what she had done, but Fraser suddenly staggered back. For one moment he just stood there, a puzzled expression on his face, then he put his hand to his nose, letting out a long drawn-out wail when he saw the blood on his fingers.

'Touch him again, Fraser, just once, and I'll kill you.'

The boy took one look at her standing there with her fists clenched and then ducked past her, his handkerchief to his nose and stumbled out of the room, sobbing bitterly.

'He's been asking for that. I don't think he'll try anything again, but if he does, just let me know.'

'What did you do to him?'

'Head butted him. My father's been teaching me unarmed combat — the stuff the commandos do.' She looked at me with her ice-blue eyes. 'It seems to work all right.' She rubbed the top of her forehead briskly and then smiled. 'There's not even an egg there to show for it.'

If that was one side of her, I thought, her behaviour in the gym the following Sunday was another. She didn't put me down by showing off and vaulting the horse herself, but explained the theory of getting enough forward momentum and allowing that to carry one over.

'Just concentrate on getting your hands as near to the far end as possible and once you do that, the rest's easy. Let's practise first with you jumping over my back — I'll get really low to start with and then gradually make it higher.'

She wouldn't let me near the horse until I was confident of leaping over her back without hesitating and when we went round and round the gym, vaulting over each other in quick succession, and, wonder of wonders, I even began to enjoy it. Finally, she drew a chalk line on the horse and even though the first few times I failed to reach it with my hands and, as I had always done before, landed on top of it, she refused to allow me to become discouraged.

'I know, we'll go round once more jumping over each other and when we get to the horse, all you have to do is imagine it's me and you'll sail over.'

To my utter astonishment, and no doubt hers as well, that's what I did. I cleared it by a good six inches and the second and third time by even more.

'You've got it. You've really got it.'

She was excited as I was, laughing and with her hair all mussed up, and then we were hugging each other and quite suddenly I kissed her. My glasses and my nose got in the way, but I, Richard Medley, who was beginning to find my mother's goodnight embraces an embarrassment, had actually kissed a girl. As Patricia stepped back when it was over, I saw that there were pink patches on her cheeks and she was breathing as if she had just sprinted a hundred yards. Then she turned and ran out of the gym.

At the next physical training period, I could sense Blackstone's anticipation at my coming downfall. The man kept glancing at me, a half smile on his face, and he left the jumping right until the end of the class, making me go last. Several of the others had failed, but Blackstone hardly said a word to them and then it was my turn. Out of the corner of my eye, I saw Patricia looking at me and pushing her hands forward in front of her and then I got into my stride. It wasn't the horse I was jumping, it was Patricia, the smooth skin of her back showing above her shorts where her shirt had ridden up and it wasn't leather that my hands came into contact with, it was the firm muscles above her shoulder blades. I cleared the horse by a good foot and without saying a word, the headmaster turned and marched out.

Was it the man's disappointment at my success, I was to wonder later, that made Blackstone behave to me in the way he had during prep a couple of nights later? I had put my hand up to ask a question and the man had stared at me for a moment and then beckoned with his forefinger. 'Medley,' he said. 'Medley, come here.'

The man's voice was quite gentle, but although I sensed that there was something wrong, I had no idea exactly what and stopped some three feet short of him, blinking at him nervously through my glasses. The head made another gesture with his hand encouraging me to come closer and then stood there stock-still, his arms hanging loosely by the side of his sharply creased grey flannel trousers.

'Come here, Medley, I'm not going to hit you. I've got something to show you.'

I sidled towards him, head bowed and taking one hesitant half-step after another, and was just shooting a furtive glance up at him when something exploded against my left cheek. I was off balance anyway and with that and the force of the blow, I fell sideways on to the floor, my glasses skittering across the boards. I was almost completely blind without them and went on to my hands and knees, feeling around for them and trying to choke back the sobs. When I finally located them, I wiped away the tears and put them back on, flinching as I saw Blackstone standing over me.

'Go back to your place, Medley, and stop snivelling.'

The man stood there, looking in turn at the boys sitting at the long tables in the assembly hall, the top of his deeply tanned bald head reflecting the light from the powerful bulb under which he was standing, then made a dramatic gesture with his hand towards me.

'You may well wonder at the sequence of events just now. Well, let me explain. Medley is, as you all know, a clever boy — he has hopes of getting a scholarship next year — but cleverness can be overdone. He has the distressing habit of asking questions to which he knows the answers. I was merely demonstrating that he doesn't know all the answers and that it is a mistake to believe everything you hear; it is necessary to employ *savoir-faire* as well. I'm sure you know what *savoir-faire* is, Medley. Would you care to enlighten us? You wouldn't? I can't say I'm surprised. How about you, Baxter? Anyone else? Keeping a low profile when the going gets a bit tricky, eh? Not such a bad idea. You're all showing *savoir-faire*, which was the whole point of the exercise. *Savoir-faire* comes from the French to know and to do, knowing how to do — know how, not, however, to be confused with that nasty Americanism savvy, which means to understand, and comes from the Spanish *sabe usted*, you know, from the Latin *sapere*, to be wise. Quite instructive that little exercise, I'm sure you will all agree.'

'Pig.'

Even though the word was hardly more than whispered and the person saying it was at a different table, I heard it quite distinctly and cast an agonized glance in the headmaster's direction.

'Did you say anything, Blackstone?'

The girl clamped her lips together and looked fixedly at her father.

'I'm waiting.'

I knew what was going to happen, I just knew it, and did the only thing I could think of to distract the headmaster. I began to sob and then to cry loudly. It might have been play-acting to start with, but it soon wasn't and I completely lost control, such that, despite all Blackstone's threats, I just couldn't stop. The man must have realized it himself, because he dragged me up to the dormitory, pushed me on to the bed and left with a snort of disgust.

I was left there alone during evening prayers, which meant that I would be able to get into bed before the others came up and pretend to be asleep. At least, that was my intention, but Miss Brice came into the washroom while I was cleaning my teeth.

'Richard, why have you come up so early?

37

Aren't you feeling well?'

I liked Miss Brice — she was young, pretty and good fun — and her look of concern was enough to set my eyes watering again.

'And what's happened to your lip?'

'Nothing, Matron.'

'You haven't been fighting, have you, Richard? That's not like you.'

She turned my face to the light and gently touched my lip with her finger.

'Poor old you. The skin is split and I'll put some antiseptic cream on it for you.'

When she came back and dabbed some on, giving me a hug, I began to cry again.

'Is it stinging badly? It shouldn't, you know.' I shook my head miserably. 'Why not tell me about it? I'm sure it will help.'

'It was Mr Blackstone,' I said between sobs.

'He hit you?'

'Yes, and I hadn't done anything. I just put up my hand to ask him a question during prep, he beckoned to me to come towards him and then he hit me across the face.'

She listened in silence while I told her what the headmaster had said afterwards, then gave me another hug.

'Cheer up, it's not as bad as all that. Now look, Richard, if he ever does anything like that again, I want you to tell me straight away.

Promise me you'll do that.'

When I did so, she wiped my tears away.

'Now, why not pop into bed before the others come up?'

I realized that she must have sensed that Fraser and his cronies wouldn't have left me alone, for she stayed in the dormitory until everyone was in bed.

'Now look, there's to be absolutely no talking after lights out and I mean just that. I'm on duty tonight and if there's so much as a whisper out of anyone, I'll tell the headmaster and you know what'll happen if I do that.'

She left the door open a crack, but even that and her threat wasn't enough to prevent Patricia from sliding out of her bed and leaning over me.

'You made that scene to protect me, didn't you?' she whispered. 'I think it was very brave of you.'

In the morning, the others seemed to have forgotten about the incident, but I hadn't and neither had Patricia. She gave me a little smile across the breakfast table and I felt like a knight in shining armour. I wouldn't have put it quite like that at the time, but I still remember the warm glow that had gone right through me.

I was able to bask in further glory with

Patricia a day or two later, when Mr Hannam was giving us a chemistry lesson.

'Does anyone know what an element is?'

After my experience with Blackstone, I was reluctant to put my hand up, but Mr Hannam was quite another proposition and gave me a smile of encouragement.

'I'm sure you know, Medley.'

'It's a substance that can't be broken down any further, sir.'

'That's right and each one of them has an equal number of atoms and protons in its nucleus — you no doubt remember that I was speaking about that last week.'

He unrolled a large chart and pinned it on to the blackboard.

'And here we have the periodic table.'

Hannam glanced at me again.

'It's the table in which the elements are put in sequence according to their atomic number.'

'You certainly seem to be in your element this morning, Medley.'

The man received an appreciative titter for that sally, but he was right. The others collected cigarette cards and knew all about football and cricket, but science was my hobby as well as part of school work. Hannam went on to explain about compounds and touched the chart with his wooden pointer.

'Arsenic has an atomic number of 33 and its oxide is a deadly poison.' With a dramatic gesture, he marched across to the glass-fronted cabinet, unlocked it and lifted down a bottle from the top shelf. 'Arsenic trioxide! As you see, it is a powder and it is used as a rat poison and weed killer, but having a faintly sweet taste and being undetectable in something such as cocoa, providing it is boiled to allow it to dissolve, it has also been used . . . ' — he paused dramatically — 'for murder.'

There was never any fidgeting or lack of attention in Mr Hannam's classes. Even those with not the slightest interest in the periodic table, or chemistry as a whole for that matter, thrilled to the story of the 22-year-old Madeleine Smith, who had been charged with the murder of her former lover in the nineteenth century.

'If you want my opinion, she not only did it, but got clean away with it and survived to the ripe old age of ninety-three. Can you imagine living for seventy years with the memory of having done something like that? Well, Baxter, do you suppose the attractive and beautiful Miss Smith ever got married?'

'Oh no, sir.'

'But she did, twice, and, what's more, outlived both her husbands.'

'How did she give him the poison, sir?'

'That would be telling, Baxter. Let me just say that she put a paste containing arsenic on a rather private part of her anatomy and that is how he came to ingest it.'

'Sir?'

'That's enough, Baxter.'

'If she was guilty, sir, how did she get off?'

'Thanks to the brilliant performance of the defence lawyer. Even so, she wasn't found not guilty, a verdict of non-proven was brought in — a peculiarity of the Scottish courts.'

It was directly after that lesson that Patricia came up to me.

'I wish I knew half as much as you, Medley,' she said. 'I'm hopeless. There's the maths test on Friday and I know I'm going to fail it.'

'You'll be all right. Is there anything I can help you with?'

She looked at me unblinkingly with her piercing blue eyes.

'You could sit next to me and pass me the answers if I get stuck.'

The cold shiver went right down my back. 'But the head's invigilating and you know what happens if anyone gets caught cheating.'

She shrugged her shoulders. 'I'll get the cane anyway if I fail, so what's the difference?'

'But he'd never do that to you, not to a girl.'

'Oh yes he would; he's done it often enough before, but you won't tell anyone about that, will you?'

'No, of course not.'

'Promise? He'd kill me if he found out that I'd been talking about it.'

'I promise.'

'Don't worry, it's not fair to involve you and I suppose I'll have to grin and bear it — I just hope that I won't have to bare it as well.'

'All right, I'll do it.'

I could have bitten my tongue off, but I was too much of a coward to go back on my word. Nevertheless, I really was in mortal terror of Blackstone and what the man would do if we were caught. In the forty-eight hours before the test, I could hardly eat or sleep, my imagination playing tricks on me as I lay in the darkness and terrifying nightmares coming whenever I dropped off.

'You look dreadful, Richard,' Miss Brice said to me after breakfast on the day of the test, 'come up to the sickbay and I'll take your temperature.'

The mercury obstinately refused to rise above 98.4 degrees so that was another escape route cut off. The temperature was the critical index of illness at Brantwood — no temperature, no illness, and even I had to admit that that rough and ready method worked well enough.

What made the whole thing worse was that the test wasn't until 5.30 that afternoon and I had to sit out classes and go through the motions of a game of football before it started. Cheating was no easy matter, either. We had to write our answers in an exercise book, which made it much more difficult to look at one's neighbour's work than would have been the case if we had used separate sheets of paper. I eventually worked out that the only way to do it would be to remove the double spread from the centre of the book by prising open the staples with the point of my compass and let Patricia have the answers on that. If I pressed them back again neatly, the missing pages would never be missed, or so I fondly hoped. The simplest parts of it were removing the paper, which I did beforehand, and doing the easiest questions twice — I knew that Patricia wouldn't be expected to cope with the harder ones — and the nightmare was passing it across.

For the first half-hour of the test Blackstone paced around and there was no chance at all of doing it, but just when Pat was getting anxious and nudged me with her knee, the headmaster went across to the window and looked out. It could have taken me no more than a second and I could have sworn that I had made no noise, but Blackstone must have seen a reflection in the glass.

'Medley,' he said, without looking round. 'What do you think you're doing?'

The man turned, his lips twitching, and snapped his fingers at his daughter, who got to her feet and held out the piece of paper without looking down.

'It was all my fault, sir. Medley didn't want to do it, but I told him before the test that if he didn't help me I would get him into trouble with you.'

Blackstone looked down at the solutions, tapping the paper with his forefinger.

'Is this true, Medley?'

My throat seemed to have closed up and my mouth wouldn't open.

'I don't tell lies, sir,' Patricia said.

'No, you don't, do you? I'm disappointed in you, Blackstone, but at least you haven't tried to make excuses. The penalty for cheating is six strokes of the cane and for helping someone to do it, is three.' He paused. 'I think it would be only fair for you to receive both punishments, don't you?'

The girl didn't say anything and still didn't

look down, but Medley could see her shivering.

'You will go up to my study and wait for me there and in view of the word you used to me the other day, which you seem to think I hadn't heard, you will wait for me without the normally accepted protection. I'm quite sure you know what I mean by that.'

Long after she had gone, the headmaster remained in the room pacing around and then stopped on the other side of the table where I was sitting.

'I dislike physical cowardice, Medley, but I dislike moral cowardice even more. You are partly responsible for what is about to happen and don't you ever forget it.'

None of us really believed that he was going to do it until the first sharp crack of the cane came through the door, which Blackstone had obviously left open deliberately. I could only ever remember one boy having got six, and that was for a severe case of bullying, but nine! I winced at every stroke, almost as if I was getting them myself, as each one followed with agonizing slowness and then at last it was over.

Patricia was the first one to reappear. Her cheeks were flushed, her breath was coming in great gasps through her nose, and her lips, which were clamped tightly together, were trembling, but her eyes were dry and Medley hadn't heard her make a sound while she was upstairs. She stood by the door, waiting for her father to come past, and when he marched through, she didn't turn her head to look at him. She closed the door carefully, then walked straight back to her place and sat down with a loud thump on the bench. I heard her grunt with pain as she did so and then glanced anxiously at the headmaster. Please God, I said to myself, don't let him do anything more to her, please!

I had seen Blackstone stiffen at her act of defiance. For a moment he stood there stroking his upper lip with his forefinger, then one of his sinister half-smiles crossed his face and he turned away. The man waited until the second hand of the clock had moved round to exactly 6.30 and then rang the bell.

'Harris! Your turn to collect the books, prayers at a quarter to and then cocoa for everyone.'

If Blackstone had gone out of the room, I would have spoken to Patricia, but I never got the chance. The headmaster now seemed to be in a particularly benign mood, moving around the room, chatting to everyone, making jokes and looking around with his alert eyes until his wife came in with the pile of hymn books. After handing them to

Reynolds to distribute, he picked up his own copy and flicked through the pages.

'Ah, yes. Not the original Bunyan, but this will do very well, I think.

> 'He who would valiant be
> 'Gainst all disaster,
> Let him in constancy
> Follow the master.'

'If one substitutes she for he and headmaster for master, we have an illustration of what happened this evening. I will not tolerate cheating, but I admire the ability to admit straight out that one has erred and even more do I admire spirit and courage and the ability to take punishment like a man. One of your number has shown an abundance of these admirable qualities this evening and one other's part in it all has been considerably less than noble. I do not think I need to labour the point any further. Margaret, your admirably nimble fingers can take care of it, can they not?'

Without looking at her husband, Margaret Blackstone found the place, put the book against the music stand and played the first line very loudly, hitting the notes as if she hated them and then wincing as Blackstone started to sing at the top of his voice, off key

48

and with total disregard of the tempo she had set.

I loathed singing, never more so than on the rare occasions that the headmaster made me perform solo, but it didn't do to appear not to be taking part, so I mouthed the words with what I hoped was every appearance of enthusiasm. Even against the loud piano accompaniment and Blackstone's raucous voice, I could hear Patricia's bell-like treble, which stood out against the others and, glancing sideways, I saw her singing for all her worth, her eyes fixed on the hymn book.

To my relief, it was Miss Brice who was supervising us again as we washed and cleaned our teeth before going to the dormitory.

'Where's Patricia?' she asked, when, apart from her, we had all got into bed.

'I think she's still in the bathroom, Matron,' said the boy who slept in the next bed to the girl. 'Do you want me to fetch her?'

'No, that won't be necessary, thank you, David, I'll go to see how she's getting on myself. And no one's to get out of bed while I'm away, do you hear?'

Since the beginning of term, Patricia had been allowed to use the staff bathroom at the end of the corridor, but it was most unlike her to be last and I looked at her anxiously when she finally did come in. She obviously hadn't been crying, though, and she gave me a little smile before taking off her dressing-gown and getting into bed.

'Everyone snug? Right, goodnight everybody. Sleep well.'

'Goodnight, Matron.'

I buried my head in the pillow, but then jerked round a few minutes later when the light came back on.

'What are you playing at, Fraser?' the boy in the next bed to him said.

'Shut up, Pedlow. The Head will be tucking into his dinner by now and we haven't seen young Blackstone's marks yet.'

'She doesn't have to.'

'We don't need advice from crybabies like you, Medley. Everyone shows their marks, even the Headmaster's precious daughter. Come on, Blackie.'

When Patricia, who was sitting up by now, didn't move, Fraser let out a loud sniff.

'I don't believe your father really caned you at all,' he said with a sneer.

'But we all heard it.'

'I bet he was just hitting a cushion to make us believe he had — she wasn't even crying and everyone cries, even after three.'

Patricia stared him straight in the eye. 'I

never cry, Fraser, not like you. You can't even take a hard tackle.'

She stood up on the bed, turned towards the wall and her hands went to the waistband of her pyjamas, which a moment later dropped down to her ankles. She lifted up the top a fraction and turned slowly first one way and then the other.

There were gasps as we all saw the lumpy, dark purple band, some three inches wide, which crossed the centre of her neat, muscular backside and the flecks of dried blood at the edges of it.

'Satisfied?' she said, looking over her shoulder.

'There's someone coming.'

The hoarse whisper from the boy on the bed nearest the door, was followed instantaneously by the light being extinguished and a flurry of movement, which stilled a moment before the door came open.

'Who switched the light on? Come on, I saw it shining under the door.'

'I did, Matron.'

'Why, Patricia?'

'I heard someone crying and thought they might be ill.'

Miss Brice sighed. 'You might at least have thought up a reasonable excuse, Patricia. Look, I'm not going to repeat the warning I gave you all the other day. If anyone gets out of bed, that light comes on again, or if I hear a single sound, the Head will hear about it. Do you all understand?'

'Yes, Matron.'

3

I tried to catch Patricia on her own the following morning, but somehow the opportunity never arose, or was it, I wondered, that she was avoiding me? That Saturday was the day of the match against Ravenscourt, our deadly rivals. I hated games, and most of all I hated football, but the whole school had to watch the Ravenscourt match, however cold it was or however hard it was raining.

My mother liked me to send her the annual school news sheet that was printed each autumn and, as it had only just come out, I still had it in my tuck box at the foot of my bed in the dormitory. Before going out to the field, I got it out and took another look at it. The contents were mainly about the happenings during the previous school year, but right at the end was a preview of the soccer season and a picture of Patricia. She was in her football kit and looked fit, chunky, fearless and formidable. Under the picture was the caption: 'Captain of football for the coming season will be Blackstone. The team will be a strong one and great things are expected of it and, it is to be hoped, a long-awaited victory over Ravenscourt after a string of defeats.'

Surely, I thought, Brantwood wouldn't have a chance with Patricia being unable to play; she had made great efforts to hide it that morning, getting up last when everyone else had left the dormitory to go to the washroom, but I had sneaked a look round the door and had seen her walking stiffly along the corridor, one hand pressed against her bottom. If she was still in that amount of pain, how could she possibly turn out for the match? Without her, we would lose and that would mean that the Head would be in a bad mood for the rest of term.

After break on Saturdays, while the others did community singing with Mrs Blackstone, I had extra maths tuition with Mr Hannam in preparation for the scholarship exam I was to sit during the next summer term. It was my best subject and I really enjoyed those classes and was pretty sure that the master did, too. I was often to wonder in later years what a man like him was doing in a prep school, although it never occurred to me to question it at the time. Hannam was not only a gifted mathematician, but was also an excellent chess player and he taught me how to play. It wasn't only that, he gave me bio-graphical sketches of all the great exponents of the game; Emmanuel Lasker, who was also a mathematician, Capablanca, the Cuban, who eventually defeated him and Alexander Alekhine, who was still alive.

We used to have speed games at the end of the lesson, which were always the high spot of the day. Hannam would lock the door, usually with a conspiratorial wink in my direction, take out his set and the genuine chess stop-clocks from the locked cupboard under the shelves with chemicals on them and we would set to. Never once did Hannam deliberately let me win and the feeling of achievement, and, more than that, triumph, when I beat the man for the first time was something I never forgot. After that, for some weeks we were evenly matched, but then I began to forge ahead.

That particular morning, Hannam was late and, as I sat waiting for him, I remembered what the man had once said: 'Chess is an excellent training for life; it teaches you to look ahead, to be patient, to watch out for traps and never to be off your guard.'

Why, oh why, I thought, hadn't I remembered that when Patricia had asked me to help her with the maths test? It was many years later before I knew the answer to that one and that was that life wasn't nearly so simple as a game of chess. It was much more difficult, largely because it was so unpredictable and emotions, which at the time I hadn't understood, were involved. If our roles had been reversed, Patricia would have helped me because she wanted to and to hell with the consequences, whereas I had only helped her because I hadn't had the courage to say no. I would never have offered to teach her to jump over the horse, but then, neither would I have dared to ask her to do anything like that for me.

My thoughts were getting altogether too uncomfortable and I got up and began to wander around the classroom. I had always been obsessively tidy and I noticed at once that the glass-fronted cabinet, which was normally kept locked, was open a fraction and that one of the bottles on the top shelf was slightly out of line. I took a quick look down the corridor and when I saw that there was no one in sight and that all was quiet, I went back. Leaving the door ajar so that I would be able to hear approaching footsteps, I climbed up on a chair and unscrewed the top of the bottle. Was the arsenic as tasteless as Mr Hannam had said? I moistened the tip of my forefinger and just touched the top of the powder with it, then licked it and ran my tongue around my mouth. It did have a taste, but not a very definite one and if I were to . . .

Blackstone was a great believer in the benefits of a good breakfast to start the day and everyone had to eat porridge. The man liked to sprinkle his liberally with salt from his special silver cellar, which was kept with the other less elegant ones in the sideboard in the diningroom. No one else was allowed to use it and although the arsenic grains were bigger, if I were to grind them up and mix them with the salt, then, perhaps ... I carefully replaced the bottle and took down the big chemistry book from the bottom shelf. I didn't understand many of the medical terms in the section on poisoning, but it was very clear that arsenic in quite small amounts would do very nasty things to people and that only a few hundred milligrams could prove fatal. I was still reading it when Mr Hannam came bustling into the room and I closed the book hurriedly.

'Sorry I'm so late. Keeping yourself occupied, I see. You won't work too hard, though, will you, Richard? There's more to life than chemistry and quadratic equations, you know, particularly when you can do the work standing on your head. You got full marks in that maths test — I corrected it last night — and that's more than can be said for young Patricia, but no doubt she will redeem herself on the football field this afternoon.'

Little did he know, I thought, what had happened to her the previous evening. That and all my other disturbing thoughts soon vanished, though, when we got down to work and the tutorial passed all too quickly for me. Hannam had just introduced me to more advanced algebra and geometry and as I had now got the hang of them, I was finding them both challenging and exciting.

Even though Patricia was at lunch and seemed to be moving around more freely, she looked pale and was unusually quiet and the last thing I expected to see when I reached the touchline just before two o'clock was her trotting out at the head of the Brantwood team. I disliked watching football almost as much as playing it as I always got chilled to the bone. Some twenty minutes later, I was shuffling about trying to get some warmth into my feet, when I heard Blackstone's familiar voice and turned to see the headmaster standing with Mr Hannam only a few feet behind and to my right.

'I don't like the look of their right wing, Edward. He's quick; he's got excellent ball control and if he sends any more of those centres over, we're going to be in really bad trouble.'

'You're right and I don't know what's got

into Pat today — he's running rings round her.'

I couldn't believe my ears. How could the man make a remark like that after what he had done to her the previous evening? At that moment, the Ravenscourt winger put a long ball past her, outdistanced her easily and centred from near the corner flag, shaking his head with irritation when the centre forward bungled yet another scoring opportunity. The next time he got the ball, he decided to cut inside with a view to taking a shot himself. Patricia Blackstone saw him start to turn, the ball at his feet, and went in flat out. Out of the corner of his eye, the boy saw her coming and tried to nudge the ball to one side, but he was far too late. They hit the ball almost simultaneously, but her momentum carried her straight into him and they hit the ground together in a flurry of limbs.

'Well tackled, well tackled indeed.' Blackstone was yelling with excitement as his daughter scrambled to her feet and cleared the ball upfield, just as the referee blew his whistle.

'What's he on about? That was a perfectly fair tackle.'

Colin Hannam pointed to the whey-faced boy, who was doubled up on the ground, trying to get his breath.

'Winded, I reckon.'

Blackstone gave a grunt of satisfaction. 'When Pat really tackles someone, they stay tackled.'

Several minutes went by before the boy was able to get to his feet and soon after, the whistle went for half-time with Ravenscourt leading by one goal to nil. As the players ate their orange segments, Blackstone ran on to the pitch and began to exhort them and then suddenly squatted down to look at his daughter's leg, rolling down her long sock and inspecting the ugly gash on her shin, which was seeping blood.

'Make yourself useful for a change, Medley,' he shouted at me 'and get some iodine and plasters from Matron.'

I needed no second invitation, running off towards the main school building, only too glad to get out of the damp and cold for a few minutes. The sickbay was one of the rooms off the corridor leading to our dormitory and I was just about to knock on the door when I heard voices coming from Miss Brice's bedroom, which was nearly opposite. I went up to it, moving carefully to avoid making the boards creak, and was just able to make out what was being said.

' . . . I dare say she deserved it and it won't have done her any harm, she's as tough as old boots.'

'You haven't seen the results of what he did to her and it's not only that, he hit Medley the other day for no reason at all.'

'There's always a reason for hitting Medley. Medley's a tick; he's a weed and a mother's boy and many's the time I've wanted to take that self-satisfied smirk off his face with the back of my hand.' His voice went up into a high falsetto. 'Please, sir, I know the answer, sir.' He always does, too. God, he makes me sick.'

'But Tony, I really believe that Blackstone's mad and one of these days something terrible's going to happen. Do you know, the other day, when I . . . '

I heard her give a sudden gasp and the springs on the bed gave a loud squeak. I tried to look through the keyhole, but the view was obstructed by the key on the inside.

'No, Tony, no . . . '

I continued to listen outside for several minutes, but then my fear of what Blackstone would do if I was too long got the better of my curiosity and I went back to the door at the end of the corridor, slamming it shut.

'Matron! Matron!'

A minute or two went by before Miss Brice appeared, looking flushed and with her hair mussed up. I had never been able to understand how the other boys could get any pleasure out of larking about and in rough-and-tumbles and surely, I thought, grown-ups didn't do that sort of thing, too.

'Yes, Medley, what is it?'

She was breathing heavily and was fiddling with the top button of her blouse, which had come undone.

'It's Patricia, Matron. She's cut her leg and Mr Blackstone's sent me up for some iodine and a plaster.'

She went back into her room to fetch the key to the sickbay and gave me a small bottle of iodine, a roll of cotton wool and a box of dressings.

'Does the Head want me to come down?'

Her voice sounded funny and she kept smoothing her skirt down.

'I don't think so, Matron.'

'Richard!'

'Yes, Matron.'

She looked at me for a moment and then walked with me right to the end of the corridor, holding the door open for me.

'It doesn't matter. Hurry along now, you mustn't keep Mr Blackstone waiting.'

The game had already restarted when I got back to the field and Blackstone snatched the things from my hand as I came running up.

'You took your time.'

Mercifully, the Head was too occupied with

signalling to the referee and then seeing to Patricia's leg to bother any further with me. The iodine must have stung her like the very devil, but apart from one sharp hiss of intaken breath, the girl didn't react at all and ran back on to the field without looking back once the dressing had been put on.

I may not have known much about football, but I knew a lot about fear and it was obvious that the Ravenscourt winger was scared stiff. Every time he got the ball, he was looking to see where Patricia was and she only had to make a move in his direction for him to get rid of it in a panic. With their best player neutralized, all the confidence went out of the Ravenscourt team. A hasty and ill-judged pass back to the goalkeeper resulted in an own goal, which equalized the score, and after that they could do nothing right.

'Well played, everyone, well played indeed,' Blackstone said, when the final whistle blew, Brantwood having won 3–1, shaking his daughter by the hand and ruffling her hair.

'It was that tackle that was the turning point. By God, you went in hard. Now run along to Matron and get that leg fixed up properly.'

I saw the man looking after her, his face shining. 'That girl, Colin, has more guts than the rest of the school put together. Now, about the swimming pool; Stacey tells me that he can't clear the drain and it looks as if we'll have to have the path up.'

'Can't it wait until the Christmas holidays?'

'I suppose it'll have to, although it's bound to smell a bit by then. Stacey's slipping — I told him to see to it in the summer holidays while I was away, but you know what he's like, if he can do a job tomorrow, he . . . '

The two men drifted out of earshot and I walked back to the main building, took *Greenmantle* off the shelf in the library and settled in my favourite corner. I loved Buchan. As I picked up the thread of the story, which I had already read twice before, I was no longer a lonely, short-sighted and deeply unhappy small boy, clumsy and no good at games, I was the mysterious, brilliant and resourceful Sandy Arbuthnot, who could pass as an Arab or Turk and triumphed in the end, despite being driven to the brink of madness by the sinister Hilda von Einem. If Sandy hadn't been daunted by appalling danger, why should I be by Blackstone? One had no need to depend on weapons such as clubs, knives and pistols, when there were more subtle ones, which I . . .

★ ★ ★

Richard Medley's voice trailed off and for the next minute or two he remained motionless, staring sightlessly at the fireplace.

'I suppose that football match was a watershed as far as I was concerned,' he said suddenly, not looking towards me and as if the lengthy pause had never happened. 'The explanation for the fact that I can recollect hardly any of the next six weeks or so, while my memory of the rest of it is so clear, must be because, for whatever reason, Blackstone began to leave me alone. I don't recall any further dramas in the dining-room, classroom or dormitory and even though I can't believe that Fraser didn't keep up his verbal attacks, it clearly left no impression on me. There's also the evidence of my letters home at that time. My mother kept all of them and when I reread those from that time a few days ago, most of the news, after my account of the football match, was about my chess victories over Hannam, the additions to my collection of cigarette cards and trivia like that.'

'How did you hear about Blackstone's death?'

'That I do remember and I shall never forget it. When the first bell went for getting up, I was fast asleep, but I don't recall anything at all unusual until breakfast. Blackstone wasn't there and neither was

Patricia, but I didn't take any particular notice of it as I was worried about having lost my glasses' case and directly the meal was over, I went outside to see if Stacey had come across it when he was tidying up in the gym. At that time of day he was always in the locker-room cleaning our outdoor shoes and as I approached it along the path leading past the gym, I heard voices. I stopped at the corner and looking round it, saw that he was talking to someone who was hidden from my view.

' "You can't mean it. Dead? Not Mr Blackstone?'

'Yes, sir. I was the one wot fahnd 'im. Lyin' face down under the thin layer of ice coverin' the pool, 'e was. Gave me a proper turn an' all.''

Stacey was full of it. How he had broken the ice, pulled Blackstone out, how he had tried to give him artificial respiration and how he had gone down to the Lodge to fetch Mr Hannam.

' ' 'E was ever so calm and businesslike. 'E said that 'e'd tell Mrs Blackstone, but not to say a word about it before 'e announced it at a special assembly, but seeing as 'ow you're a senior member of the staff, sir, I thought . . . ''

'Who was the other man?' I asked Medley.

'Mr White; I'm quite sure about it. Even

though they walked away and I didn't actually see him, I recognized him from his accent. I expect you remember it yourself; it's difficult to describe, but it didn't sound quite English somehow — Fraser told us he was a German spy!'

'Whatever made him say that?'

Medley laughed. 'Because the man used to wear galoshes and he had read somewhere that that was a dead giveaway. Anyway, I started towards the locker-room to see if by any chance I had left the case there, when I heard a sound from the gym. It was a frightful high-pitched wail, that quite literally sent a shiver right down my spine. When I looked in there, I saw Patricia sitting on one of the benches near the wall bars with her knees drawn up to her chest; her head was bent forwards, she was rocking to and fro and that dreadful sound was coming out of her.

'Why did I slink away without letting her know I was there? Why didn't I take her in my arms and comfort her? I think the answer must be that I had got so used to staying in the background and trying to remain anonymous, so used to hearing that I was a crybaby and that I must learn to control my emotions, that perhaps I felt that Patricia, the one person who never cried or showed signs of distress, would not have wanted to be discovered like that. Or maybe it was yet another example of my cowardice.

'I never saw Patricia again. Mr Hannam addressed the rest of us in the big classroom later that morning. 'There had been a terrible accident', he said. 'The Headmaster must have slipped on the ice on the surround of the swimming pool in the blackout when he was doing his nightly round, hit his head and fallen into the water'.

'I don't remember what happened during the few days before we were sent home early for the Christmas holidays — I suppose we must have gone through the motions of some school work. My mother's scrapbook wasn't much help; all it said was something like: 'After the tragedy at Brantwood, I was fortunate to be able to get Richard into the Junior School at Cheltenham for the two terms before the scholarship exam. He was very happy there and won the top award that summer. Well done, Richard, your father would have been proud of you.'

'My mother was right. Surprisingly, I was happy at both the junior and senior schools. I say surprisingly because I had heard horror tales about public schools, both from Blackstone and from Pedlow, whose elder brother was one of the senior boys when I first went to Brantwood.'

'Wasn't Pedlow that very fat boy whose bed was by the window?'

'That's right. I suppose he was the closest to a friend I had at Brantwood, Patricia excepted, largely because he, too, was always being picked on by Fraser, being the other swot in our form. We wrote to one another for a bit, swapping scholarship boasts — he got one to Winchester. Anyway, I was in mortal terror of initiation ceremonies, bullying and beatings from other boys at my new school, which I was assured I would have to endure, but none of it was true. It was my good fortune that a new broom had been appointed a few years earlier, a young headmaster who had swept away many of the old and barbaric customs — most importantly, prefects were not allowed to use the cane. Of course, there were times when I felt homesick and was unhappy, but in the main I flourished there.

'My housemaster took the view that every single boy had it in him to succeed at something, even if it was only trying to do one's best. In his eyes, and hence the eyes of everyone else in the house, academic skills were every bit as important as athletic ones, and in the end I had as much status and kudos as the captain of cricket when I won a scholarship to Cambridge. Although Mr

Meredith wasn't an academically bright man himself — he taught mathematics to some of the lower sets — he nevertheless clearly didn't resent my superior skills and, more than that, delighted in them.

'"You have great intellectual gifts, Richard', he said to me when, at the age of eighteen, I went to say goodbye to him, 'and I have every confidence that you will make a great contribution to science in the future.'

'Did he prove right? Well, it's true that I did get a first in both parts of the Natural Sciences Tripos at Cambridge, I qualified in medicine and a PhD, a fellowship at King's, an FRS and finally the Chair of Physiology at University College all followed, but a great contribution, no. I was too obsessional for that, I lacked the necessary imagination and I was not a good head of department. True, I did make some original observations in my field, but throughout the later stages of my career there was the sour taste of unfulfilled potential.'

'You're being very hard on yourself.'

'No, I'm not, just realistic. I've always been mainly on the side of genes in the nature/nurture debate, but I've never in my life been so unhappy as I was at Brantwood and I can't help thinking that it had something to do with the man I became. And what was that? Touchy, obsessional, occasionally acid-tongued and friendless is the answer. No, I'm not exaggerating or touting for sympathy, it just happens to be true. I suppose my main motive for the visit to the health farm was to try to exorcise some of the ghosts, but it didn't work.'

He opened his briefcase and took out a glossy brochure.

'I picked this up at the office there and when I saw Patricia's name on the list of directors, my memories of her as a person came flooding back. She and I were not friends in the sense of sharing confidences or anything like that, but we helped each other in so many ways. I am not a patient person — I was always a much better scientific investigator than teacher — and yet I had the patience of Job when helping Patricia with school work. For her part, like her father, she despised physical and moral cowardice and yet she seemed to understand mine, did her best to protect me from the bullies, including her father, and helped me with gym work and stuff like that. In one way, I would love to see her again, but in another . . . '

I could see how embarrassed he was as he pulled his handkerchief out of his pocket and made a rather unconvincing display of blowing his nose.

'I've never been any good with girls, or women for that matter and I . . . '

His voice trailed off and he took off his glasses and began to clean them with great care.

'You wouldn't want to say or do the wrong thing, or perhaps spoil your fond memories of her? Is that right?'

He glanced up with an expression of relief and looked so like the wretched small boy I remembered so well that I spoke without thinking.

'Would you like me to see if I can contact her and try to get some sort of impression of her? There would be no need for me to mention your name.'

His reaction was immediate. 'Would you? Would you really? I realize that you must be very busy and there's no hurry, but I would be most grateful.'

'May I keep this brochure?'

'Of course.'

'And you don't happen to have either that photograph or the news sheet you were telling me about, do you?'

'Yes, they're both here in my briefcase. I thought it might interest you to see them so I took them out of one of the scrapbooks.'

After he had gone, I went for a long walk and by the time I got back, any doubts about my offer to Richard Medley had evaporated. Why had I never gone back to take a look at Brantwood myself? After all, the place was quite close to Chichester. Frank would have said with a laugh that it was all due to deep Freudian repression hiding dark secrets and he might well have been right. However that might have been, though, my own memories were beginning to come back even more strongly and what had been a trickle became a flood when, after supper, I picked up the photograph and in my mind went back to that autumn of 1944.

4

When I was eighteen, I was certainly not lacking in self-confidence and the thought of working as under-matron at Brantwood held no great terrors for me. I was used to boarding-school, having been to one myself for five years, and, first as a prefect and then as head girl, I also knew about keeping order and although I had had no contact at all with small boys — in fact boys of any sort, being an only child — I didn't suppose that they were all that different from small girls. My interview with the headmaster went well, too, which got me off to a good start.

'Good, excellent,' he said, when I told him that I had played hockey and cricket for my school. 'I don't suppose you'd be averse to helping out with a bit of coaching at those games, then, would you?'

'No, I would enjoy it.'

'Capital. I can see that we're going to get on splendidly. Don't worry about lack of experience, just let the little devils know who's boss right at the outset and you'll be all right. The ability to command respect and discipline is a difficult quality to define, but I know it when I see it and I see it in you.'

I was extremely flattered and without false modesty knew that what Blackstone had said was true. I remembered the teacher who had arrived at the beginning of my last term at school and I had felt it within seconds of her coming into the classroom. The wretched woman just hadn't got it and predictable chaos had ensued before the first period was half over. The noise had soon attracted the attention of Miss Fairbank and that was the other side of the coin; the deputy headmistress was a mild enough looking woman, but she only had to put her head round the door and order was restored — just like that.

Edward Blackstone and the whole school, for that matter, had impressed me when I had been shown round at the time of my interview, but within a few days of starting I discovered that there were large cracks behind the façade. To begin with there was the headmaster's wife, Barbara. I had been told that the woman was the official matron, but it soon became clear that she had no intention of undertaking any of the duties involved. I was the one who had to supervise the boys' getting up and going to bed, who dealt with the minor complaints, helped the doctor with his weekly visits and organized the laundry and regular changes of clothes.

Barbara Blackstone was very much younger than her husband and it was a conversation that I overheard some two weeks after the start of term that revealed something of their strange relationship. I had gone down from the dormitory one evening to tell the Head that one of the radiators was leaking slightly, hoping to catch him before he started his evening meal. The door to the dining-room was ajar and I was just about to push it open further, when I heard his voice and hesitated.

'On form again, I see, Mrs Stacey.'

Through the gap by the jamb of the door, I saw him take hold of the large glass dish from the cook through the hatch.

'Thank you, sir.'

I was just beginning to turn away, having decided to wait until after he had finished his supper, when I heard the hatch close with a crash.

'Edward, if you say that once more, I shall scream.'

Going back to the door, I saw Barbara Blackstone, her face like thunder, staring at her husband, who went on with the task of giving himself a generous helping of shepherd's pie and sprouts without looking round.

'I say it because I mean it and people like to be shown a bit of encouragement. I don't suppose I can tempt you, my dear.'

'Are you becoming a mind-reader, or something? I can just about put up with prep-school food for lunch every day, but exactly the same thing for dinner is more than I can stomach. I've already eaten, if you must know.'

Blackstone opened the bottle of Worcestershire sauce and began to shake drops of the brown liquid all over the food, followed by a large sprinkling of garlic, which I had already noticed that he added to almost everything he ate.

'In that case, to what do I owe the pleasure of your company?'

'I want to talk to you about Patricia.'

Blackstone cut a sprout carefully into two, dipped it into a puddle of sauce and chewed it carefully before swallowing.

'Oh, you do, do you?'

'Yes. She's too old to be in a dormitory with a group of boys. She's twelve and a half and no longer a child.'

'Patricia is perfectly happy as she is and if there's one thing that upsets anyone at school it's being different from the others.'

'But that's precisely the point — she is different from the others.'

'I don't think so. She's the best and most courageous back I can remember here, she has spirit and integrity and she's as happy as a sandboy. Surely you can see that.'

'Since when was being a good soccer player a desirable attribute in a girl? Patricia is a girl, Edward, a fact that even you can hardly deny any longer, even though you've been trying to do so ever since I've known you.'

'Patricia has the use of Miss Brice's bathroom this term and she'll be able to keep an eye on her.'

'She still has to share a dormitory with eleven boys. Has it not occurred to you that a girl rapidly approaching puberty needs privacy, not to mention the company of other girls of her own age?'

'I do not require a lecture on Patricia's welfare, least of all from you, Barbara, and I hope you haven't forgotten our bargain. Now, much as I have been enjoying our little discussion, Mrs Stacey will be wondering what's happening.'

He pushed his plate to one side and reached for the silver bell, which was standing next to the pepper mill, but before he could ring it, his wife snatched up his plate and pushed it and the two dishes back through the hatch.

'What on earth's that?'

'Bread and butter pudding, madam.'

'I can see that, Mrs Stacey, I'm not blind. I was referring to that stuff you've sprinkled on top of it.'

'It's Mr Blackstone's special tablets — he prefers it if I grind them up and he likes to take them that way.'

Barbara Blackstone let out a sigh and carried the plate across to her husband, putting it down heavily on the mat in front of him.

'What is it this time, Edward? Surely you're not putting garlic on your puddings as well as everything else. I would have thought that even you would have balked at such a combination.'

'Don't be ridiculous, Barbara. It's zinc.'

'Zinc?'

'Yes. It's good for virility and you needn't look at me like that, Barbara; may I remind you that virility means a good deal more than your narrow understanding of the word? It also means strength, forcefulness and vigour, all of which one needs in abundance doing a job like mine.'

Blackstone rapidly finished his pudding and then dabbed his lips delicately with his napkin.

'Are you ready for your drink, Edward?'

'Yes, thank you, my dear.'

I saw Mrs Blackstone go to the cupboard by the side of the hatch, take out a tin of chocolate and mix several teaspoonfuls of the powder in a mug of milk, which she handed

79

to the cook to be heated.

'Beautifully done as always, my dear,' he said after taking a sip. 'Mrs Stacey always makes it too weak.' He put the mug down carefully on the table. 'Miss Brice seems to be settling in well, don't you think?'

'She's certainly a great improvement on that half-wit from the village you employed last term.'

I tiptoed away and up the stairs back to the dormitory where Patricia and the older boys slept. I wasn't in the habit of listening at half-open doors and was still feeling guilty about it as I made sure that everyone had washed properly. As I came out of the bathroom, I saw Patricia striding down the corridor, swinging her dressing-gown cord and whistling quietly to herself.

'Done your teeth?'

'Yes, Miss Brice.'

'Good.'

The girl gave me a smile and walked confidently into the dormitory, hung up her dressing-gown and got into bed. She certainly looked happy enough, I thought, as I turned out the lights and she was clearly brimming with health and vitality. The conversation I had overheard outside the dining-room explained a lot. I had thought Mrs Blackstone very young to have a daughter of Patricia's age and hadn't been able to understand her almost complete detachment from the girl. The fact that she obviously wasn't her mother and must be Blackstone's second wife went some way to explaining it, but what had the man meant by their 'bargain'?

'All quiet, Miss Brice?'

I hadn't heard the headmaster's approach and whirled round.

'Yes, sir. They're all in bed and I've just switched the lights out.'

'Splendid. Quite settled in now, are you?'

'Yes, thank you.'

'Capital. You're doing very well, very well indeed. Keep it up.'

I was to think later that I ought to have noticed much earlier on how extraordinary Blackstone's behaviour was in many ways, but I was otherwise occupied, having just discovered sex. I had known the biological facts and a good deal more than that for years. My father and my school, for that matter, had been pretty good about that sort of instruction and when I was sixteen, I also discovered an old and dusty volume in the bookcase in my father's consulting-room at home.

It was its title *Psychopathia Sexualis*, that first attracted my attention, but what really heightened my interest was that most of the 'naughty bits', to use the parlance of my grandchildren, were in Latin. It didn't occur to me at the time to question why it was there at all — I assumed that every GP would have books like that — but later on, I knew that they didn't. I strongly suspect that my father had a considerable interest in the wilder shores of sexual activity, no doubt to compensate for the lack of any hint of response from my mother in that direction, who shied away from any physical contact with me and, I have no doubt, with him as well. She was one of those people who disliked being touched and more than once I saw the hurt expression on my father's face when she brushed aside his attempts to give her a hug or a kiss. Had he sought consolation elsewhere? Later on, when I knew a great deal more about male sexuality, I thought it more than likely, but if he had, it was done with the utmost discretion.

Thanks to Richard von Krafft-Ebing, I was unusually well-informed on sexual matters for an 18-year-old girl of that era and that book also did wonders for my Latin. While, though, I might have been strong on the theory, my experience of the practical was not just weak, it was negligible. Years later, when I was in general practice, I was often to think that there were many worse ways of starting off than with what we used to call 'heavy petting'. There was a code in my social milieu, for most boys as well as girls, which said so far and no further and that lasted pretty well until the sixties and the advent of the pill. It had so many advantages, I thought. It showed you how your body worked; there were no risks of pregnancy or disease; there wasn't the degree of commitment to which a full sexual relationship frequently leads and, above all, with the right partner, it was fun.

It had nothing to do with love and luckily for me, Anthony Jarrett, the young English master, viewed it in exactly the same light. I didn't feel the merest glimmer of guilt, but I did have one reservation and that was a major one. Anthony liked, as he put it, 'a bit of spice and pickle', and although that didn't mean that he wanted anything physical that was in any way unacceptable to me, it was the circumstances in which he wanted it that worried me.

On one occasion, when everyone was assembled in the big classroom to listen to one of Churchill's broadcasts, we were standing behind everyone else and Tony slipped his hand up under the back of my dress. I tried to fight him off, but my movements caused the boards to creak and that brought a disapproving glance from Blackstone, who was sitting a couple of rows in front of us, and when I kept still, the sinuous fingers began to creep upwards. I remember having fixed my gaze on the headmaster's bald head, I did my best to concentrate on the broadcast and when that didn't work, tried to imagine what life was going to be like at medical school, anything to arrest the now familiar feelings which were beginning to build up. When it came, I couldn't help myself; I had to react in some way and pretended to sneeze, which provoked another angry look from the headmaster.

'If you ever even try to do anything to me under circumstances like that again,' I said to Tony afterwards, 'that'll be the finish. I really mean it.'

I did mean it at the time, but our games had become almost an addiction and Tony managed to manoeuvre me into taking crazy risks. Luckily for us, we had such a close call one evening that it even sobered Tony Jarrett. We were taking a bath together and he did something with a bar of soap that was making me let out a series of half groans and little cries, when someone hammered on the door.

'What's going on in there?'

'I'm just having a bath, sir. Did you want anything?'

'I thought I heard voices.'

'I was just singing to myself, sir.'

I heard Blackstone move away and whispered urgently in Tony's ear. 'He'll wait in the corridor until we leave, I know he will. You'll have to go out by the window.'

'Like hell I will! It's freezing out there.'

'But he'll catch us and then we'll be thrown out.'

'Who cares? Its none of his business and there are plenty of other jobs available.'

It wasn't so much losing the job that I was worried about, it was what my father would think and say.

'Please, Tony!'

When he shook his head, I did the only thing I could think of; I pretended to burst into tears.

'Oh, all right then.'

Luckily, the window opened easily and quietly and the climb down was relatively simple as there was a lean-to shed against the wall directly below the bathroom. I made absolutely certain that no incriminating evidence of Tony's presence had been left behind, readjusted the blackout curtain and went out into the corridor. As I had feared, Blackstone was hovering at the end of the passage and even though he didn't say anything apart from a muttered goodnight, I left the door of my bedroom open a crack and saw him go into the bathroom and seconds later heard the sash window going up.

If I was scared of Blackstone, then the boys were even more so and some, like Richard Medley, were in mortal terror of him. I knew perfectly well that small boys thought nothing of lying in order to curry sympathy, but Medley hadn't lied about being hit by the headmaster for no reason, one of the others confirming his story in every detail. Medley, I thought, was the type of boy for whom a boarding-school must have been an utter misery, particularly one run by a man like Blackstone. Although tall, he was slightly built, short-sighted, timid, a bit of a know-all and one of the two cleverest boys in the school, all of which added up to his being the perfect victim for the bullies.

A few weeks later I knew that something out of the ordinary must have happened directly the first boy came up after prayers and that finally convinced me that not only was Blackstone seriously disturbed, but that something ought to be done about him.

'You seem very excited about something, Simon.'

Walker, the youngest boy in the dormitory, was obviously dying to tell me all about it and the words came out in a rush.

'Blackstone got the cane during the maths test.'

'Not Patricia, surely not Patricia.'

The boy nodded his head vigorously. 'She got nine.' He looked round. 'And she was made to take her shorts and pants down, too.'

'Don't exaggerate, Simon.'

'I'm not, Matron. The Head told her to go up to his study and we all heard what was happening through the open door.'

Patricia seemed perfectly all right when she came up and I still didn't believe the boy, but when she went along to the bathroom and fifteen minutes later hadn't reappeared, I walked along the corridor to see how she was getting on. The door was slightly open and through the gap, I saw something that pulled me up short. The girl was standing with her back to the mirror, her pyjama bottoms around her ankles and she was looking at herself over her shoulder. She was a great deal more physically developed than I had expected, but that was something I only noticed in passing, my attention being riveted by the parallel purple, almost black bruises disfiguring her backside. Even more extraordinary than that, though, was the expression on the girl's face as she gently drew her finger across the corrugated ridges on her skin: she was actually smiling to herself.

I stepped back and went along to the dormitory. For once, I had difficulty in quietening everybody and could hear them talking after I had switched the lights out. After what had already happened, my worry was that Blackstone would come up and I gave a shiver at the thought of what might happen if he were to do so. I allowed them a few more minutes' grace, but when I came out of my bedroom a little later and saw that someone had switched the light back on, it was Patricia who owned up to having been responsible, giving me some feeble excuse. Threats of the headmaster seemed to do the trick, but even so, I waited outside until I was quite sure that they were at last well and truly settled.

What should or could I do about Blackstone? I was still thinking about it when I went into my bedroom the following afternoon. The trouble was that there was no one with whom I could discuss it. Old Dr Franklin was so ancient that he wouldn't begin to understand what I was talking about, not to mention the fact that he had known Blackstone for years and clearly respected him; my father would tell me that interfering would only make matters worse and Tony would laugh at me. He did laugh at me. He tapped on my door just as I was trying to forget about it all by starting a letter.

'I'm busy and anyway I don't feel like it this afternoon,' I said, when he put his arms around me.

'Oh, come on. It's the best opportunity we've had for ages. I know you think that Blackstone's got his eye on us the whole time, but you know as well as I do that nothing's going to take him away from the Ravenscourt match.'

I tried to explain my worries about the man and how he had beaten his daughter and hit Medley, but predictably he refused to take me seriously.

'But Tony, I really think he's mad and that one of these days something terrible is going to happen. Do you know, the other day — '

We were facing each other and quite suddenly he pushed me down on to the bed and began to tickle me.

'No, Tony, no . . . '

I meant it when I said it, but I was just as frustrated as he was when we heard Medley calling from outside in the corridor and the spell was broken.

I kept a special eye on Patricia after that, but she seemed her usual bouncy self until, not long after, she came up to the sickbay during morning break.

'Excuse me, Matron.'

'Yes, Patricia, what is it?'

'I think I've hurt myself.'

'Where?'

'I'm bleeding.'

It took a moment or two for the penny to drop and then I went up to her, put my arm around her shoulder and gave her a hug.

'It's nothing to worry about. It's quite normal and it happens to all girls when they grow up. Hasn't your mother explained?'

'I haven't got a mother.'

I was appalled and after I had fixed her up, I arranged a time with her and we had a long chat. Poor little thing, she was almost totally ignorant and what ideas she did have about sex were curious in the extreme. So curious, in fact, that had it not been for my mentor Krafft-Ebing, it would never have occurred to me even to consider, let alone to suspect that Blackstone might have been responsible for her strange beliefs. Why on earth, I wondered, hadn't someone, her stepmother or the school doctor for example, spoken to her about periods and at least warned her about what was going to happen? Perhaps, though, I thought, it wasn't quite so strange as it first appeared. Blackstone clearly thought of her as a son, he and his wife obviously had a most peculiar relation-ship and Patricia equally obviously resented her stepmother. As for Dr Franklin, he was so far past it that he hardly knew what day of the week it was. Apart from all that, plenty of other girls in that era were left in exactly the same boat as Patricia, even those with mothers and older sisters.

I knew that I ought to have had a word with Barbara Blackstone about Patricia, but I kept putting it off, not having the confidence to face the woman whom I found distinctly forbidding. Eventually, my chance came when I was playing the piano in the music-room one afternoon when the boys were on the games' field. I had had lessons at school for many years and I enjoyed working at it. One of the problems of being an all-rounder, though, which I think I can fairly claim that I was, was that there wasn't enough time to become really good at anything, not that I am trying to claim that I had any special talent for the piano. The peak of my efforts had been to play a Schubert impromptu at the school concert during my last term. It was the only piece of any length that I had ever learned by heart and, to my surprise, I got through it again that afternoon without any major hiccups, despite not even having sat at a piano for several weeks.

'I didn't know you played.'

I gave a sudden jump and turned round.

'I'm sorry, Mrs Blackstone, I didn't hear you come in.'

She gave me a smile and it suddenly struck me that it was just about the only time I had ever seen her do so.

'You're clearly no beginner, but would you mind if I made some suggestions? At the moment, you're trying to play the piece too quickly and, as a result, you're missing out quite a few of the notes. The arpeggios must be rapid, but also light and very clear. May I show you?'

In the next half-hour, I learned more about that piece than in all the weeks I had struggled with it at school.

'Why not work at it on those lines,' she said, 'and you can play it to me again next week. Remember to practise it slowly, the fireworks can come later. It would also be a good idea to start something new. Have you ever tried any of Brahms' intermezzos?'

'No, I haven't.'

She opened one of the drawers in the music stool and pulled out a book.

'Have a go at this one — the notes in it are not too difficult.'

She played it for me and it was immediately obvious that she was in a different class from my previous teacher — she was really good. When she had finished it and I had thanked her, I decided that I might never have a better opportunity to tackle her about Patricia.

'Mrs Blackstone?'

'Yes.'

'I wonder if I might have a word with you about Patricia.'

'Patricia?'

Her tone of voice made it quite clear that the shutters had come down and with a vengeance, but I wasn't going to be put off that easily.

'Yes. Her period has just started for the first time and she obviously wasn't expecting it. I showed her how to cope and did my best to explain things to her, but . . . '

The woman nodded. 'I'm sure you did it very well and I'm very grateful to you.'

'But — '

'Shall we meet here at the same time next week?'

The subject was not mentioned again despite the fact that I saw the woman regularly at my weekly piano lessons, when she talked animatedly about music and seemed to take a real interest in my progress. In any case, by that time I wasn't too worried; slowly but surely Patricia began to relax with me and to talk about this and that, largely the trivia that teenage girls like to share, and during those times, I think we almost became the sisters that neither of us had had and would have liked. Everything else seemed to be settling down, too, but it must have been about three weeks later, that I first began to notice that there was something wrong with Blackstone. The man looked unwell, his skin was dry and he was clearly not enjoying his food with the same relish as before. It was not long after that that he came up to the dormitory one evening when I was expecting the boys to appear after their cocoa.

'I wonder if you'd do me a small favour, Miss Brice?'

'Yes, of course, sir.'

'I'd like you to come down to the dining-room at precisely seven-thirty. The door will be open, but don't come in, wait outside, listen and perhaps even observe what happens, but on no account allow yourself to be seen.'

I was so flabbergasted that all I could do was stare at him in amazement.

'What about the boys?'

'Mr White will cope with the boys: he will be coming up any moment now and you can tell him what to do. Are you absolutely clear in your mind about my instructions?'

'I think so, sir.'

'Thinking is not enough. Repeat them to me, please.'

I did so and seeing Blackstone close to for the first time for quite a few days, I was shocked by his appearance. He almost seemed to have shrunk; the skin on the top of his head, which at the beginning of term had been tanned and so shiny that it reflected the light, was now dry and scaly and there was a puffiness around his eyes that I hadn't noticed before.

I had had very little to do with David White, the French master. He was a slight, very pale-complexioned man, whom I judged to be in his early twenties. He had a shock of curly black hair, which contrasted with the other members of the male staff, all of whom had short, neat cuts, and he spoke with a faint but distinct accent, which I was unable to place. He always looked tired and I remembered once having gone into the masters' common room to look for Blackstone and saw White staring out of the window. As I went in, he turned and, to my amazement, I saw that tears were running down his cheeks. I had absolutely no idea what to do — I had never seen a grown man crying before — and in my embarrassment, I apologized for disturbing him and backed away. That evening, he seemed even more preoccupied than usual and clearly wasn't listening when I told him what to do, so much so that I thought he must be ill.

'Are you feeling all right, Mr White?'

His eyes suddenly focused on me. 'I'm sorry?'

I went over Blackstone's instructions again in my mind and, glancing at my watch and seeing that it was only a couple of minutes before 7.30 hurried out of the dormitory and down the stairs. What on earth was going on, I wondered? Blackstone was clearly physically ill and mentally, too, for that matter. I decided there and then that I would have to speak to Dr Franklin about it at his next visit, but before that, what was in store for me outside the dining-room? I didn't have to wait long to find out. I saw Blackstone sitting at the table facing me and his wife's voice came from out of sight.

'Aren't you going to finish your pudding, Edward?'

'I haven't got much appetite.'

'Your hot chocolate, then?'

'You wouldn't want me to do without that, would you, Barbara?'

'Not if you enjoy it and it helps you to sleep.'

'Very well, then.'

As she came into view and began to busy

herself at the hatch, I saw Blackstone following her every move with his eyes and when she had finished preparing the hot drink and put it down in front of him, he made a gesture with his hand.

'Sit down for a moment, would you, my dear?'

The woman gave a slight shrug of her shoulders and then did so.

'I've not been feeling myself recently.'

'I've been telling you for weeks that you look unwell and you've refused to do anything about it. Why don't you go to see Dr Franklin? You can be very stubborn, you know, Edward.'

'Franklin is an old fool. I did go to see him and all he did was give me more bromides.'

'No wonder your skin's so dry.'

'There's another possibility and I think a more likely explanation for that, Barbara, and that is that someone is poisoning me.'

'Don't be ridiculous, Edward.'

'The only item of food or drink that I neither prepare myself, nor share with others, is my nightly hot chocolate.'

'Edward, you're sicker than I realized.'

'If the suggestion is as ridiculous as you suggest, why don't you drink it yourself?'

'You know how much I dislike the stuff.'

Blackstone smiled. 'Not a very convincing

excuse. Tell me, why do you want me out of the way?'

Barbara Blackstone shook her head, went across to fetch the tin, added another couple of heaped teaspoonfuls of the powder, stirred the mixture vigorously, then picked up the mug and very slowly drank the contents before putting it down again on the table with a loud bang.

'There, does that satisfy you?'

She made a move to get up, but he reached out and took hold of her wrist.

'No, it does not. You would not be beyond making yourself vomit on leaving here. You will sit next to me for the next hour and if you do not . . . '

'If I do not?'

'I will have no alternative but to call in the police.'

I waited there for perhaps ten minutes and then could stand it no longer. My last sight of them was of Blackstone, his watch resting on the table in front of him, staring fixedly at his wife, while she sat perfectly still looking straight in front of herself.

I heard the noise when I was only halfway up the stairs leading to the corridor where my bedroom was situated. It was a regular thumping sound. As I came round the corner, not only was it clear that it was coming from the dormitory, but just outside the door, I could just make out David White. The man was hunched over, his shoulders were shaking and a low keening sound was coming out of his mouth.

'Are you ill, Mr White?'

He stared at me and then shook his head, pointing towards the closed door. I had heard from Tony that the wretched man couldn't keep order and I suspected that things had got completely out of control.

'Why not come and sit in the sickbay for a moment?'

White could hardly walk and I had to support him as we went back along the passage.

'Wait here a moment, I won't be long.'

As I approached the door of the dormitory, I heard Fraser's voice, instantly recognizable as his was the only one to have broken.

'Ve vill not tolerate die spies in our midst. Achtung! Zey rooted out must be.'

I opened the door quietly and saw Fraser striding around the room doing the goose step. He had stuck a piece of the flap of an envelope blackened with ink above his upper lip, had combed his hair in a parody of Hitler's style. As I watched, he came to a halt in front of Medley and gave the Nazi salute.

'Heil myself! Vat haf you to say?'

'Leave him alone, Fraser.'

As Patricia took a step towards him, Fraser suddenly saw me and all the colour went from his face. I had never been one to lose my temper easily, but I still had a vision of the wretched man cowering in the corridor in my mind's eye and something snapped. I ripped the piece of paper from the great bully's face and, big though he was, got hold of his ear and gave it a vicious tweak, holding on to it and pulling him towards his bed, until he overbalanced and fell on to it, where he lay clutching the side of his head and crying.

'Get into bed the lot of you. You ought to be ashamed of yourselves.'

I think they must have been aware that I was close to losing control completely and was capable of anything. They scurried away like a lot of frightened rabbits, burrowing under the bedclothes and while I walked up and down the only sound was the snivelling coming from my left. Without saying another word, I switched out the light and stalked out of the room, leaning against the wall of the corridor until my heart had stopped pounding.

White was sitting on a chair in the sickbay, his elbows on his knees and his face buried in his hands and, as he looked up, I saw his expression of utter misery and distress. I was completely out of my depth, already shaken by the events outside the dining-room and dormitory, and what I did next was pure instinct. I took the poor man in my arms and hugged him, rocking him backwards and forwards, comforting myself every bit as much as him. I had never been one to cry easily and on top of that it had been discouraged at my boarding-school, but I couldn't control myself then and, curiously enough, that seemed to help him. After a few minutes, he took out his handkerchief and dried my eyes.

'Don't distress yourself,' he said, his voice still shaky. 'I'm all right now. You were a great help and I'm very grateful, more than I can say.'

He took my face between his hands, looked at me for a long time and then gave me a sad little smile, kissed me on the forehead very gently and left the room.

I was so upset by what had occurred that I neither put two and two together, nor did I even speculate about the reason for White's collapse; in fact, if anything much else had gone wrong in the next couple of weeks, I think I might well have cracked up completely, or run away, but mercifully nothing did. Blackstone, who was looking rather better, never alluded to the events in the dining-room, Fraser gave me a wide berth and White, who had previously ignored me more or less completely, started to give me little smiles of recognition whenever he passed by. I really thought that all the trouble was over until that piercingly cold morning in the first week of December when, after having got up at the usual time, I hurried along the unheated corridor to the bathroom and found it locked. Apart from me, Patricia was the only other person who ever used it and I knew that it must be her inside.

'Are you in there, Patricia? You won't be long, will you? Patricia, are you all right?'

When there was no response, I was just thinking that I would have to break the door down in case she had collapsed when I heard the key being turned in the lock. The girl looked absolutely terrible; she was in her pyjamas, as white as a sheet, shivering and had obviously been crying.

'What's wrong, love? Aren't you feeling well?'

When she didn't reply, merely shaking her head, I took off my dressing gown and put it round her shoulders.

'Come along. There's a bed made up in the sickbay and I'll get you a nice hot water bottle.'

When I went in with it a few minutes later,

Patricia had at least stopped shivering and I bent over the bed and gave her a kiss.

'Will you be all right here for a few minutes? I'll come back when I've got the boys up and you can tell me all about it. Don't look so scared, I'll only be just along the corridor.'

Had it really been more of a struggle to get everyone going that morning, or was it just my faulty recollection of all that time ago? I don't think it was the latter; there is nothing like strong emotion to fix memories and there was plenty of that floating around that morning. Unusually for him, Medley was fast asleep — normally he was the first one up — and Fraser hung about refusing to get into the cold bath, which they all had to have every morning. I was just about to shout at him when I caught sight of the reason, which he was making a rather ineffectual effort to hide with his hands. Poor fellow, he was well into adolescence and I had neither the common sense nor the experience to understand why he had started to hate appearing naked in front me. Luckily for both of us, it was at that moment that I heard a voice from the corridor outside.

'Miss Brice!'

'Yes, Mrs Blackstone.'

The woman motioned to me to follow her

down the corridor.

'Where is Patricia?'

'In the sickbay. She's not feeling at all well this morning.'

'What's the matter with her?'

I hadn't the remotest idea and said the first thing that came into my head.

'Just the time of the month, I think.'

'Oh!' She looked at me unblinkingly. 'Mr Blackstone has had an accident — Stacey found him in the swimming pool a short time ago.'

'But . . . '

'He's dead, Miss Brice, and someone is going to have to break the news to Patricia. No, don't worry, I'm not going to ask you to do it for me, I just want you to get all the boys down to breakfast as quickly as possible.'

The sickbay was empty by the time I had returned and I went down the stairs. There were voices coming from the staff-room near the front door and, not wanting to interrupt, I went outside and glanced through the window. I could see Hannam and Barbara Blackstone talking to Dr Franklin and just as I was wondering what to do next, I heard a dreadful wailing sound coming from the direction of the gym that sent me running along the path by the side of the house.

Somehow I managed to calm Patricia and

took her back to the sickbay, staying with her and talking to her until Dr Franklin came up and gave her a sedative. I was still sitting by her side when there was a soft tap on the door. I found Mr Hannam standing outside and I left the room, closing the door softly behind myself.

'Is she all right?' he asked.

'She's asleep now.'

'I'm glad about that. Her uncle is coming down from Malvern to fetch her this afternoon. Do you think you could pack some of her things?'

'Of course, but — '

'Don't worry, it's the best solution under all the circumstances. Mr Gerald Blackstone and his wife are very nice people; they know Patricia and I'm sure they'll look after her well. Are you all right yourself?'

'Yes, thank you.'

'Good. I'm afraid that the next few days are going to be very busy. I have decided to end term early and I'll start contacting the parents right away — may I rely on you to supervise the packing?'

I suppose that I must have switched off in some sort of way and, in any case, I had far too much to do to have had the time to think about the circumstances of Blackstone's death. It was Hannam who saw me off a week later when the taxi came to take me back home.

'You've been a real tower of strength,' he said. 'I don't know what we would have done without you. Good luck in your future career.'

'Don't you want me back next term?'

'I'm afraid there's not going to be a next term; the school will be closing.'

An outsider looking at it would probably have thought it strange that I was not more upset by what had happened and by my having to leave the school, particularly after my heady experiences with Tony Jarrett. The fact that I wasn't, showed, I suppose, that the relationship had never had any real depth and was, in any case, by then beginning to lose its freshness and spontaneity. What said it all was that in the mad rush at the end of term, we didn't even exchange addresses and later on, neither of us took the trouble to find out each other's whereabouts.

And so there was no great drama as far as I was concerned once the dust had had a little time in which to settle. I was young, there was the future to look forward to and what with Christmas, the job I obtained at the local hospital, the excitement of the end of the war in Europe and my move to London, I was soon able to put all those bizarre events firmly out of my mind.

5

It took me a long time to get off to sleep that night after my meeting with Richard Medley. Not only was I excited about what he had told me and also by my own memories, but I was also appalled when I came to think about what had gone on at Brantwood School. Why hadn't I or anyone else done something about it at the time? Even though I was half asleep, I realized at once the futility of viewing the situation as it was then with hindsight and the benefit of over half a century of experience. After all, I had only been eighteen then, the social scene had been totally different and the headmasters of small privately owned preparatory schools, who were not answerable either to trustees or boards of governors, were, within very wide limits, laws unto themselves.

The war also had a great deal to do with it. Apart from the fact that there were no half-terms, nor, except in exceptional circumstances, even visits to the school by parents, fathers of the majority of the boys were in the forces and mothers were struggling to keep homes together. Was it therefore so surprising that they had had no time to question the eccentricities of a man like Blackstone, even if they knew about them, which quite possibly they didn't? There could be no denying, either, that in many ways the school was a success considering the difficulties. The boys were kept as warm as fuel restrictions allowed; they were well fed; they were an exceptionally healthy lot and a glance at the list of scholarships and common entrance successes on the boards on the walls of the big classroom had been proof of academic excellence.

The more I thought about the whole business the following morning, the less did I feel inclined to tackle Patricia Blackstone straight away. It was partly due to the feeling that she might not wish to be confronted by an echo of the distant past, but also that I wanted to find out a great deal more about her father's death before doing so.

Blackstone himself obviously thought that he was being poisoned and I had myself observed some of the signs, which I hadn't recognized at the time, but that I now knew were consistent with arsenic intoxication and, on top of that, there was Medley's extraordinary account of the bottle of arsenic trioxide. What was a poison like that doing in a cupboard in Hannam's classroom, which the man had so casually left unlocked, and why had he told the boys in his form the story about Madeleine Smith in all its prurient detail? If Medley's recollection of that had been accurate, and his account had had the ring of truth about it, it could surely not have been a coincidence, and if it wasn't, did it mean that the man had been trying to incite the boy to poison Blackstone and if so, why? Arsenic, I also knew, could produce a disorder of the peripheral nervous system and that might well have made Blackstone unsteady on his feet, particularly in the dark. Could that have been the reason why he had fallen into the swimming pool?

How to set about looking into events which were more than fifty years old? It was as good as a tonic for me to have to use my brains and even more of one to have been able to find some useful information almost straight away. An extremely helpful woman at the Public Library gave me a book on do-it-yourself genealogy, which told me where to look for details of death certificates, inquests and wills and, having driven the short distance to Midhurst, I spent some time looking through the files of the local newspaper. It wasn't difficult to pinpoint the date of Blackstone's death to within a day or two of the beginning of December 1944 and

I soon found the relevant paragraph and copied it out.

TRAGIC ACCIDENT AT LOCAL SCHOOL
Edward Blackstone, owner and head-master of Brantwood School, was found dead in the school's swimming pool early yesterday. It is thought that he must have slipped on a patch of ice and fallen in during his usual nightly round of the premises. Mr Blackstone was a respected figure in the local community, being a prominent member of the Home Guard and numerous charitable committees. He leaves a widow and a young daughter. An inquest is to be held shortly.

There was a short entry a couple of weeks later about the inquest, which merely reported that the coroner had brought in a verdict of accidental death by drowning.

Normally, going up to central London is something I avoid as far as possible, but for once I was looking forward to it and the following morning I went there by train and visited The Family Records Centre, which gave me access to Blackstone's death certificate and a copy of his will. The former was interesting enough, the cause of death being given as drowning, with a head injury, epilepsy and a condition, tuberous sclerosis, that I had just heard of and knew nothing about, as contributory factors. Equally intriguing, if not more so, was his will, which he had made only four weeks before he had died. He had left his wife a lump sum of £2000 on the understanding that she didn't contest the will; if she did and it proved unsuccessful, she would get nothing. The school and the rest of the estate in its entirety went in trust to Patricia until she attained the age of twenty-five. There was only one other item and that was that his body should be given to the National Neurological Centre in London for research purposes.

I went to see my solicitor the following day and showed him the notes I had made.

'Very interesting,' he said. 'The fact that the will has been proved means that it wasn't successfully contested.'

'Why do you suppose that was? I thought that wives couldn't be left out like that.'

'Being bequeathed that amount is hardly being left out — two thousand pounds was a considerable sum in 1944, perhaps the order of fifty thousand in today's money. Times were very different then, too, and the Inheritance Act, which deals with family and dependents, was only brought in in 1975. I see that Morton and Brookes of Midhurst was the firm of solicitors involved and I might be able to dig up some more information from them — one of their partners is my regular squash opponent. I'm afraid, though, that there will be a charge.'

'I didn't imagine for one moment that there wouldn't be.'

Alan Bristow allowed himself a wintry smile. 'I'll drop you a line when I hear anything.'

Knowing solicitors, that was going to be quite some time, I thought, and decided to try my luck at the Neurological Centre. My son, Paul, had worked there as a senior house officer as part of his general medical training and it was quite likely, I thought, that he would be able to advise me how to set about it.

'Playing the detective now, are you, Ma?' he asked when I had explained about Blackstone.

'You could say that.'

'Good for you. Well, in most hospitals you wouldn't have a snowball's chance in hell of finding any notes going back as far as 1944, but they're very proud of their records at the Neurological Centre, especially in the Department of Pathology, and if the body was given for research, particularly with such an obscure condition as tuberous sclerosis, there should be a copy of the autopsy report at the very least. I tell you what, why don't I have a word with Weldon? He's the senior physician there and he owes me a few favours — I've been looking after his wife's chronic bronchitis for years and a right old misery she is. I suppose I ought to have some credible excuse for asking; any suggestions?'

'You could say that I'm writing a history of Brantwood during the war, or if that doesn't sound convincing, prep schools in general.'

'You devious old thing!' He gave a chuckle. 'What a good idea! It's just the sort of thing that might intrigue someone of his generation. Why don't I give him a ring straight away?'

'But I couldn't ask you to do that.'

'Why ever not? No time like the present.'

Paul was achingly like Frank, I thought. He had the same bounce and decisiveness and the near compulsion to do things, whatever they were, at once. Something in my expression must have told Fiona, my daughter-in-law, what I was thinking, because she leaned across, put her hand on mine and gave it a gentle squeeze.

'No problem,' Paul said, when he came back. 'As luck would have it, Weldon's currently the chairman of the medical staff committee there and he's not only happy to give you the authority to look at the old records, but he's also going to have a word with Henderson, one of the pathologists, who indexed all the old autopsy reports some years ago and is also in charge of the department's museum.'

The arrangements all went like clockwork and a week later I went in through the main entrance of the Neurological Centre's research block and was directed to the pathologist's office on the fifth floor. Alastair Henderson was a large, rumpled-looking man; his white coat, the pockets of which were weighed down by an assortment of notebooks and small bottles, had a large coffee stain on one sleeve and I noted with quiet amusement that one of his socks was inside out.

'Dr Weldon explained about my interest in Edward Blackstone, I hope.'

'Yes, he did and quite fascinating it has turned out to be.'

'So you do have some information on him?'

'Indeed I do. You see, during the war, with the exception of a token out-patient department here, this hospital was moved down to Sussex and old Dougal McKay, who was the father of neuropathology in this country, came back from retirement to help out. Sir Henry Rawlence had been seeing the patient for a number of years and it was he who

114

made the clinical diagnosis in the first place, but it was thanks to McKay that the notes were preserved and the specimens mounted.'

'So you have some of the clinical notes as well.'

'Yes. Perhaps you'd care to look at them first and then I'll show you the pathology. I've just got to look at some urgent smears from the operating theatre, so you're very welcome to use this office and I'll ask Helen to bring you in a cup of coffee, if you like.'

'That would be most kind.'

There were two sets of notes. One lot was in a thick, bound volume with Sir Henry Rawlence's name and the dates 1935–1939 on the cover and was the record of Blackstone's in-patient investigation in 1938 and the other a couple of typewritten sheets, which were a transcript of the out-patient entries, most of which dated from the war years.

The illness had started with a couple of major fits in the early part of 1938, when Blackstone was thirty-seven. I knew very well that epilepsy arising for the first time at that age was often of serious import and that was the reason why the man had been admitted for investigation. It was then that the diagnosis of tuberous sclerosis had been made. The condition didn't rate a mention in the one textbook of medicine that I kept at home, but despite my ignorance of it, I did know about epilepsy and it was obvious that to start with that had been the major problem and it wasn't until he was put on bromides that complete control was finally established. The in-patient notes were extremely detailed and it was quite clear that there had been no hint of mental instability at that time. Reservations about his behaviour were first mentioned in a note dated February 1944.

Long rambling diatribe about his wife's real or imagined infidelity, the note read. *Is planning to put a private detective on to her. Is this the first sign of a frontal tuber?*

The last entry was made at the end of November 1944 and read:

He looks unwell and his skin is very dry. He is convinced that he is being poisoned and he may well be right — by the bromides! He has not had a fit for over two years and I have suggested a very slow reduction in the dosage.

I was deep in thought when the door opened with a crash and Henderson backed into the room carrying a couple of large pots in his hands.

'How have you been getting on?' he asked, putting them down on the floor behind his desk.

'Tuberous sclerosis is a closed book to me, but I do know a bit about bromides, which were still in use as sedatives and anticonvulsants when I first qualified, but were discontinued soon after.'

'Yes. There was a splendid rumour, which was still going the rounds when I was doing my national service, that the powers that be were putting it in the army tea to damp down the libidinous impulses of the common soldiery and from what I remember of the taste of that terrible stuff, there may have been some truth in it.'

I gave a chuckle. 'At least I was spared that. I am aware that the drug could produce skin rashes, but do you know if it also could give rise to mental changes and paranoia?'

'To be honest, I'm not sure, but in this case there were other more likely explanations for that state of affairs.'

'The tuberous sclerosis?' The man nodded. 'I'm very much in need of a tutorial on that.'

'I can't say I'm surprised; neurological rarities are our stock in trade here, but even so, we don't see all that many cases of it. It's a most interesting condition that has an autosomal dominant inheritance.'

'And that means that any child of an affected parent, male or female, stands a fifty-fifty chance of getting it, doesn't it?'

'Not quite. Penetrance is not complete, so the risks are quite a bit less than fifty per cent and one also sees very mild forms of the condition in affected relatives. I won't bore you with a long lecture on the disease, suffice it to say that it affects predominantly the skin and the nervous system, although other organs may be involved.' He lifted one of the pots off the floor. 'Now, you can see from this horizontal section of the man's brain that in his case, the tubers, called that because of their root-like appearance, are almost exclusively in the frontal and temporal regions of the brain. They are a form of tumour, if you like, and they may turn malignant, but hadn't done so in this case.'

'And their position would explain his uncertain behaviour?'

'Indeed it would. There is a most interesting case recorded in the French literature in the 1980s of a man in his thirties who started to exhibit mildly sadistic behaviour in a sexual context, never having done so before. He also had fits and died following a severe one when he was on the job, so to speak. He was found to have a fronto-temporal tuber at post-mortem.'

That made me sit up, all right. 'Do you happen to know what sort of behaviour?'

'Beating his girlfriend with a cane. I should

add that according to the report she was an enthusiastic and willing participant in the fun and games.'

'I see. What about the other specimen?'

Henderson lifted up the other pot. 'As you can see it's the man's left foot to show the small benign fibroma under the big toenail, which is another characteristic of the disease.'

'It says in the notes that the skin of Blackstone's face was very dry; is there any mention of that in the autopsy report?'

'Let's see now.' He ran his finger down the typewritten sheet. 'There is a comment here that there was no evidence of adenoma sebaceum, which is one of the more common dermatological manifestations of the disease, and in that condition, the skin is usually more greasy than normal. Wait a moment. Yes, it says here: 'skin on scalp and forehead dry and scaly'. Why do you ask?'

'I saw from the notes that Sir Henry Rawlence put it down to a side effect of the bromide medication, but Blackstone thought he was being poisoned and I believe he was right. To my certain knowledge, the man's skin was perfectly normal until only a few weeks before his death, which surely wouldn't fit in with the bromide theory and from what you've said, the tuberous sclerosis would, if anything, have had exactly the reverse effect.

Seeing that second pot has also given me an idea of how it might be proved.'

'You've lost me I'm afraid.'

'Something I heard the other day makes me think that arsenic might well have been the culprit and if I remember correctly, it both gets into and stays in the nails. Would it be asking too much to have a paring analysed?'

Henderson rubbed his nose reflectively. 'It would certainly be possible and what you have said intrigues me more than somewhat, because there was something else in the autopsy report, which I was reviewing in the light of your visit, which didn't fit in with the conclusion either that the man had a fit and then hit his head on falling into the swimming pool, or else slipped on the ice and did the same thing. These days, coroners are often loath to allow general pathologists, let alone specialist ones such as McKay, to do full post-mortems in cases of accidental death, or those occurring under suspicious circumstances, but during the war it was a different matter. McKay, like most neuro-pathologists, was no great forensic expert and you also have to remember that with the notable exception of Sir Bernard Spilsbury, specialist pathologists of that type were very thin on the ground at that time.

'In this case, there were a number of shortcomings in the way the autopsy was done. In the first place, there isn't a full description of the state of the lungs, so no evidence is presented that the man drowned, even though that was McKay's conclusion, and secondly, there is a report here and even a sketch of a depressed fracture of the skull. McKay was a more than competent artist and I do not see how having an epileptic fit and falling into a swimming pool, admittedly with a thin covering of ice, could possibly have led to an injury of that sort. A linear fracture of the skull would have been perfectly possible, but not a marked depression on the very top of it.'

'If neither a fit nor a fall would fit in with that type of fracture, what do you think would?'

'I did quite a bit of forensic work before I took up neuropathology and in my experience that type of injury is almost invariably the result of a blow from a blunt instrument. Don't get me wrong, I'm not being critical of McKay; it's only too easy to be wise after the event and one has to remember, too, that he was well past retirement age at that time. Knowing the man's reputation, I'm quite sure that he would have been very excited at finding a case of tuberous sclerosis — you can see that from the way the notes, slides and these pots have been prepared — and he would have no doubt concentrated on that side of things.'

'Do you think that the blow on Blackstone's head would have been severe enough to have killed him?'

'I very much doubt it. It's quite clear from the report that there was very little underlying brain damage.'

'So it's likely that he did drown?'

'I would think so, even though, as I said, all the evidence isn't there.'

'Would you be able to get that nail analysed for me? I'd quite understand if you say no.'

'I don't see why not. It wouldn't spoil the specimen and it could do with being remounted. There is one condition, though.'

'What's that?'

'That you let me know the full story when you've unravelled it.'

I laughed. 'If I unravel it. Of course I will and I'm really most grateful to you for all your help.'

Henderson rubbed his hands together. 'Think nothing of it, something like this does wonders in relieving the daily grind. Give me a ring next week and I should have something for you by then.'

While I was waiting for that and to hear

from my solicitor, I had plenty of time in which to think. Sooner or later I was going to have to face Patricia Blackstone, unless, of course, I decided to call the whole thing off and let sleeping dogs lie. What chance would she have had of turning out even reasonably normal after an upbringing like hers, and how well would her uncle have been able to cope with her following her father's death? Considering the way that the will had been drafted, I presumed that Barbara Blackstone would have had nothing more to do with her and yet, despite all that, Patricia had obviously made a success out of Brantwood as a health farm. I wasn't just going on the glossy brochure, either, knowing how mis-leading they could be, but also on what my GP, Alan Parfitt, had said.

'You're not thinking of going, I hope?' he asked, when I asked him if he knew anything about it.

'No, but a friend of mine in London is and I promised to make some enquiries. Why, what's wrong with it?'

'Nothing, provided you've got money to burn.' He laughed. 'I'm not being fair, really, just envious. What gets my goat is that they have magnificent facilities, which are only open to the extremely well-heeled, show-biz types, who can afford to pay the earth for two to three weeks of 'stress relief therapy' as they call it.'

'What exactly do they do?'

'Oh, they take up whatever fad is currently going the rounds. Meditation, hypnosis, saunas, jacuzzis, flotation chambers, mud baths, reflexology, aromatherapy, you name it, they've either got it or tried it. Recently, they've begun to jump on the athletics injury bandwagon. To go with that image, they have now expanded the physiotherapy service, provided by young women, most of whom appear to have come straight off Bondi beach, not to mention the odd piece of beefcake to satisfy the rich dowagers. There's an excellent cuisine for those who want to opt out of the carrot juice and nut cutlet régime. Put all that together and you have a sure-fire recipe for success, particularly if you make it outrageously expensive. It's also been established for long enough to have become something of an institution — I'm surprised you've not heard of it.'

'I don't move in those circles.'

'Neither, to be honest, do I. The only reason I know about it is that I saw an article on health farms in *Country Life* in which it featured and I couldn't resist going to have a look.'

After hearing all that, I was sorely tempted

to have a snoop myself, but decided that that would have to wait. What I really needed to do first was discuss the whole affair with someone whom I could be satisfied had not been involved in Blackstone's death and yet who would understand the background and who had known the people at the school. When it came down to it, apart from Patricia and Medley, the only ones who qualified and who might still be alive were Barbara Blackstone, White and Tony Jarrett. A little more reflection narrowed it down to one; not only had I never managed to get close to Barbara Blackstone, she certainly wasn't off my list of suspects, either, and I had hardly known White. As for Hannam, he must surely be dead by now on the grounds of age alone.

To my surprise and considerable amusement, I found myself blushing at the memory of Tony Jarrett. What, I wondered, had happened to the man to whom I owed so much? That was really true; at that time, our experiments together had been the most exciting experience of my life; they had given me great pleasure and had been both educational and enormous fun and with the ever present fear of Blackstone catching us at it, there had been the additional spice of danger, all without us having gone the whole way.

I hadn't the first idea about how to set

about tracing him and it was Paul who came up with the answer straight away.

'Still on the trail, eh, Ma?' he said. 'What you need is a private eye.'

'Who? Me? I wouldn't know where to find one and even if I did, I most certainly wouldn't trust him.'

'Relax. I'm not about to suggest that you wander around Soho looking for a chap wearing a fedora and with a mid-Atlantic accent. I know just the woman for you.'

'Woman?'

'Don't sound so surprised, Ma. We are in the twenty-first century, you know. She happens to be a patient of mine and I got talking to her about her job. Tracing people is her speciality; men defaulting on maintenance payments, children snatched by one parent, missing persons — you name 'em, she finds 'em and all with the minimum of fuss. Don't start thinking either that she's some dollybird with cascades of blonde hair and a see-through blouse; Pamela Wainwright looks just like an income tax inspector, which is exactly what she used to be.'

Two weeks later, I was kicking myself for not having thought of the way of doing the job myself, particularly as Richard Medley had found me by using an almost identical method. Once I had told the woman that

Tony Jarrett had been at Cambridge at the beginning of the war, even though I couldn't remember, or hadn't known the name of his college, all she had to do was make a few phone calls and there was his address obtained from the register of old alumni of Downing College.

Any lingering doubts I may have had about going to see Tony were dispelled when I rang Dr Henderson for the results of the analysis of the nail and when eventually I heard from Bristow, my solicitor. I decided against writing to Tony, not wanting to risk a polite refusal to see me, so, as a start, I rang up my cousin who lived near Torquay and when she said that she would be only too pleased to see me and that I could stay as long as I liked, I took it as a good omen and set out in my trusty Astra.

The Sea View Private Hotel suggested either the faded gentility of the *Separate Tables* variety, or possibly something like *Fawlty Towers* but neither quite fitted the bill, although the former was closer to the mark. The receptionist was a healthy-looking young woman, who looked up as I came in.

'Yiss. Can I help you, madam?'

'You're from New Zealand, aren't you?'

I saw at once that I had made a friend for life.

'How did you know? I'm usually taken for an Australian.'

'Local knowledge. My husband and I went on a tour of both islands eighteen months ago.'

We chatted for a minute or two longer and I then asked if Tony Jarrett was in.

'I think he's in the lounge, madam. I'll go and see if you like. Who shall I say it is?'

'Janet Brice from Brantwood. Be sure to say the Brantwood, won't you?'

Tony Jarrett must have been all of seventy-nine, but he certainly didn't look it. Although his hair had thinned, he hadn't lost his trim figure, nor the twinkle in his eyes. In fact, smartly dressed in tan slacks and a blue blazer, he had more than a passing resemblance to the major in *Fawlty Towers*.

'Janet! Well, well, well, after all this time.'

He took both my hands in his and, to my utter astonishment, at least as far as I was concerned, I found that some of the old electricity was still there.

'Let's see if I can rustle up a cup of tea and then you can tell me what's been happening to you.' He found us a quiet corner in the lounge and I told him about my career and life since Frank's death.

'How about you?'

'Oh, I stayed in teaching. I got a job at

Blundell's after I left Brantwood and remained there until I retired. Not exactly adventurous, was it, but I can't complain. An old aunt left me some money and rather than live on my own, I've found a cosy little niche here.'

'You never married?'

I regretted the question as soon as I had posed it, seeing the twist of his lips and the raised eyebrows.

'No, I didn't — never found the right person.' He suddenly laughed. 'My God, we had some good times at that funny old place, didn't we?'

'We certainly did.'

'Now, I don't suppose that after all these years you took the trouble to seek me out and come down all the way from Chichester just to renew our fun and games, although one can always hope.'

I decided to let that one pass, explaining how and why Richard Medley had come to see me.

'That's what started it all off. I had a look at Blackstone's death certificate and his will, one thing led to another and I became absolutely convinced that the man had been murdered.'

'Tell me more.'

'Blackstone thought he was being poisoned

and he was quite correct.'

'How on earth do you know that?'

I explained how I had been witness to the extraordinary scene in the dining-room between Blackstone and his wife.

'It wasn't only that. Richard Medley told me in detail about the way that Hannam had described the poisonous properties of arsenic and he freely admitted that he had got as far as taking the bottle out of the cupboard in the classroom before putting it back. On top of all that, looking back on it, I remember that Blackstone was definitely not himself in the weeks before his death — he had skin trouble, he was off his food and he had lost energy. The final piece was put into the jigsaw when I discovered that he had left his body to the London Neurological Centre.'

He listened intently while I told him about Henderson, the pathological specimens and the tuberous sclerosis.

'But I still don't see where the arsenic comes in.'

'I knew that if taken over a period of time, arsenic becomes deposited in the nails and I asked Henderson if he could arrange for a paring of one of them to be analysed.'

'And it did show arsenic?'

'It did indeed.'

'But it obviously didn't kill him.'

'No, it seems more than likely that Blackstone did die as the result of drowning, but Henderson was also convinced that the injury to his skull wasn't caused accidentally. There was a depressed fracture and a small cerebral haemorrhage underneath, both of which convinced him that it had been caused by a blow from a blunt instrument.'

'I see. But why wasn't that considered at the time?'

'It was wartime, the pathologist was old and had no forensic experience and no one even raised the question of foul play.'

'Well, all that sounds pretty convincing, I must say, and if you're right, the vital question must be were the poisoner and the blunt instrument wielder one and the same, or not?'

'Exactly. I blithely told Richard Medley that I would sound out Patricia to see if she would be prepared to see him, but . . . '

'You wondered if she might have been the one to strike the fatal blow in view of the way that her father had treated her?'

'Yes, particularly as I discovered her that morning locked in the bathroom, frozen stiff. I took her to the sickbay, but for some reason, soon after that she went down to the gym, which is where I found her sobbing her heart out — no, wailing would be a much better description. That was one of the most extraordinary things about it; according to Medley, Patricia never cried, not even when her father beat her so savagely for cheating in that maths test. She's the obvious suspect, but then I had a sight of Blackstone's wills and I wasn't so sure.'

'Wills?'

'Yes. A record of the final one was in The Family Records Centre in London and that of an earlier one was amongst his solicitor's records.'

'When did he change it?'

'About three weeks before his death. It must have been very soon after that episode I witnessed between him and his wife over the hot chocolate. In the earlier will, made in 1941 directly after he married for the second time, he had left the school to Colin Hannam and the rest of his estate to Patricia with the income going to his wife during her lifetime.'

'And the second?'

'Barbara Blackstone was left two thousand pounds and the rest of the estate went to Patricia to be kept in trust until she was twenty-five.'

'Including the school?'

'Including the school. And, what's more, Blackstone went to considerable lengths to make sure that his instructions were followed. His brother was appointed as Patricia's guardian and also one of the trustees, the others being his solicitor and the bank, and on top of that, there were affidavits from the vicar, the school doctor and a Harley Street specialist to the effect that he was of sound mind at the time the various provisions were drawn up.'

'I see; very interesting. What I can't understand is why Blackstone should have left his wife anything at all considering that he appears to have been convinced that she was poisoning him.'

'I suppose it's possible that his suspicions were allayed by the fact of her having drunk the hot chocolate that evening without suffering any ill effects and perhaps he also wanted to make sure that she didn't contest the will. My solicitor thought she might have been successful had he left her nothing.'

'My goodness, you have been busy.'

I could see from his expression that he was poking fun at me, just as he had all those years ago when I had told him about Blackstone's violence towards Patricia and Medley, but having come all that way, I wasn't going to be fobbed off that easily and put on my best crestfallen expression.

'I was rather hoping to discuss it all with

you in case you remembered something I'd missed.'

'It was a very long time ago and anyway I've got a memory like a sieve.'

'Memory is a very funny thing and, as I've found over this whole business, it's quite remarkable what comes back when you relive it, particularly if emotion, such as fear, was involved. I can remember every detail of that bath we took together and I bet you can, too.'

He gave me a roguish grin. 'Yes, I do seem to recall a little game with soap involving a submarine going into its pen and you shoving me out of that window. I never told you, did I, that Hannam happened to be walking past as I came down off that shed?'

'No, you didn't. What did he say?'

'Not a lot, just: 'Evening, Jarrett, birds'-nestin', are you?''

For the first time since Frank had died, I got a fit of the giggles, which drew a disapproving sniff from a prim-looking woman sitting in the corner, which only served to set me off again.

'I liked Hannam,' Tony said, when I had at last got control of myself. 'He may have had his moods and drank too much, but when the poor fellow was able to forget his war experiences, he could be good fun.'

'There, you see, it's all beginning to come back, isn't it?'

'It certainly is. I tell you what, I'll do a deal with you. Come out to dinner with me tonight at The Palace and I'll do my best to help you tomorrow. We might even have a dance for old times' sake.'

I could have said that I had nothing to wear, which was true, or that I was tired after my long drive the previous day, which was also true, but I didn't.

'It's a deal.'

'Capital. Where are you staying?'

'With my cousin in Babbacombe.'

'Right, I'll get hold of a car and driver and pick you up if you give me the address.'

'You'll do no such thing. What's my car for?'

I may have felt tired then, but after a short snooze and a bath, found myself really looking forward to the evening.

My cousin was able to lend me an attractive white blouse to go with a full-length black skirt and, even though I say it myself, I didn't look too bad. Tony, dapper in his well-cut suit, greeted me with a corsage of a single yellow rose and after he had pinned it on, gave me a kiss and then stepped back.

'Janet, you look an absolute picture.'

If there's one thing I'm reasonably good at,

135

it's telling whether people are being sincere and he was; he really meant it, grey hair, wrinkles and all. For me, and I think for him, too, that evening was magical. The dinner was excellent, we danced decorously and skilfully in a way that would have had my granddaughter rolling about with mirth, but which we found both nostalgic and delightful and then afterwards . . . Afterwards, Tony directed me to a spot overlooking the sea and we gazed through the windscreen at the moon lighting a path across the water.

I had thought that side of my life was over permanently, not only because of my age, but because of feelings of disloyalty to Frank whenever thoughts of 'that sort' had entered my head, but that evening I discovered that it wasn't, not by a long chalk. Tony couldn't have managed it more skilfully.

'Why don't we get in the back?' he said. 'I've always found that gear levers get in the way. Only joking,' he went on, obviously sensing my embarrassment. 'Don't worry, I'm long since past it, so far gone, in fact, that I'm even Viagra-proof, but whether or not I'm also Janet-proof remains to be seen.'

I was just able to make out his wicked grin in the moonlight and smiled back.

'Do you remember that time when we were listening to Churchill's speech in the big classroom?' he asked me when we were comfortably settled.

Did I remember it? I closed my eyes hearing again those sonorous phrases and that one particular and quite deliberate mispronunciation when the Prime Minister said 'the Nar-zee Jest-a-po'. It had been just at that point, all those years ago, that Tony's fingers had begun their insidious and remorseless progress up my leg and . . . it was the first time that I had really been able to let myself go since Frank's death and Tony seemed to understand, holding me tightly until it was all over.

6

Ridiculous though it was, I couldn't prevent the blush from spreading up my cheeks when I met Tony Jarrett the following morning, but he affected not to notice and made a gesture towards the French windows.

'I've organized some coffee in the conservatory where we won't be disturbed. The resident moggy and I are the only ones who ever go in there — it's too draughty for the old trots here — and we won't be disturbed. I suppose you'd like to know how I came to be at Brantwood and not on active service? Well . . . '

★   ★   ★

I went up to Cambridge in the autumn of the year that the war broke out. I knew that my mother had worked hard to get me declared medically unfit, but it was not a subject that was ever raised between us and I certainly wasn't complaining. She had lost two brothers in the First War and was quite determined not to lose her only son in the Second. While it was true that I genuinely did have asthma, it wasn't all that bad and if I kept away from roses, to which I was acutely sensitive, I wasn't seriously troubled by it.

In my last term at school, it could hardly have been a coincidence that my mother should suddenly have produced a particularly fine bloom with a penetrating scent and pinned it to her coat while we were waiting to see Sir Humphrey Grafton, the eminent chest physician, in his rooms in Harley Street. I had a spectacular attack there and then; so spectacular that I had to be admitted to the Brompton Hospital as a matter of urgency. Grafton, who hadn't actively treated an attack of asthma, or for that matter, any other form of medical emergency, for years, was so shaken that there was never any question but that I would be declared medically unfit for military service when the time came.

It was in September 1942 that I joined the staff of Brantwood School, the previous English master, I later discovered, having had to retire to the relief of everyone. The man had become so forgetful that there had been a number of complaints from parents and, in any case, Blackstone wanted some help with the cricket. It was that, as much as anything else, that gave me the job. There were two women in for it as well, both with better qualifications than me and with lengthy teaching experience as well, but once the headmaster heard that I had played cricket for Repton and my college at Cambridge, it was no contest.

Although the school was isolated and transport almost non-existent, the other members of staff were agreeable and I enjoyed the teaching, the boys being for the most part bright and responsive. What made the first year really pleasurable, though, was Blackstone. The man was an original. He seemed to have inexhaustible energy and was always thinking up activities to entertain the boarders at weekends. There were treasure hunts in the grounds, assault courses to be negotiated and his special lectures with slides. In his youth, Blackstone had been a keen walker and climber, both in the Lake District and the Alps, and he had many spectacular photographs and stirring tales to tell of his travels.

And then there were the films he used to show on Saturday evenings, which were not boring ones with a moral, but tales of war, adventure stories or costume dramas. The fact that there was always a long pause between each reel and the projector kept breaking down didn't spoil the fun in the least, even adding to it. I enjoyed them myself unreservedly. The films were excellent, none better than *The Thirty-nine Steps* and *The Prisoner of Zenda* and there was Madeleine Carroll to fuel my adolescent fantasies, which is what they were. I may have been 22 at that time, but I might as well have been 15 for all I knew about girls. I was an only child; I had been to a single sex public school, and both at Cambridge and at Brantwood had spent virtually all my time in male company. All that meant that I hadn't even kissed a girl, at least not properly, and my sole experience of the way they were made was through art books and the photographs of native women in *National Geographic Magazine*.

Blackstone's daughter, Patricia, was also someone who was distinctly out of the ordinary. If I had been told in advance that a girl was living and working with the boys in the school, I would have been horrified, but I had to admit that she fitted in as well as anyone. She was a likeable, happy child, as tough as nails and, in appearance, with her very short haircut and being dressed identically to the others, I would have defied anyone to have picked her out as being a female. Apart from that, she had wonderful, hand/eye co-ordination for an 11-year-old, which is what she was when I first saw her playing hockey, the game on the school curriculum during the Easter term. The grass pitch was so uneven that the others could hardly hit the ball at all, but she had no such difficulty, stopping it, dribbling and striking it effortlessly.

Colin Hannam, the deputy headmaster, who was responsible for teaching mathematics and science, went out of his way to be friendly and soon after my arrival, invited me down to the lodge at the entrance to the grounds, where he lived alone, for a drink.

'This used to be the gatehouse of the old mansion,' he said. 'The whole place was pretty derelict when Mr Blackstone senior bought it just after the First War. Property was dirt cheap then, but it still must have cost a pretty penny to convert and put the grounds into proper order for a school.'

'Have you been here long yourself?'

'Since the very beginning. Although Edward is five years younger than me, he had just missed the First War, which is how we came to be at Oxford together and when I hadn't any real idea what I was going to do when I went down, he persuaded me to come here to the school his father was in the process of starting.' He laughed. 'I never thought then that I'd still be here twenty years later.'

'This war must have made things difficult.'

'It's not been too bad. Having done my stuff in the first one and being the wrong side of forty when this one started, I wasn't called up, and both Edward and White were both unfit for various reasons. We therefore retained the nucleus of the teaching staff and with Barbara Blackstone coping with the music and doubling as matron, we have managed without too much difficulty. It also helped that Stacey was over military age. His wife has proved a pillar of strength on the domestic side with the help of various girls from the village.'

'Did Mr Blackstone senior teach?'

'No, he was bursar and ran the whole business side until his death in 1939. How about you? How come you've managed to evade Armageddon and come to sunny Sussex?'

I told him about my asthma and how I had seen the advertisement in *The Times Educational Supplement*.

'Well, I hope you'll be very happy here. You don't happen to play either golf or chess, do you?'

'The first passably — I play off twelve — and the second rather weakly.'

'Life is looking brighter every minute. I'm a shaky eight at golf; how about a game on Sunday? It's Edward's turn for church parade, as he will insist on calling it.'

I enjoyed that round immensely and the

many others I played with Colin Hannam during the year. The man, a stocky figure in his plus fours, didn't hit the ball very far, but he was extremely steady and deadly around the greens and usually won, but I had the occasional purple patch and sometimes managed to turn the tables.

If Hannam was good company and easy to talk to, David White, the thin, pale young man who taught French and History, was quite another matter. He had an aura of melancholy about him, which was hardly surprising, I thought, as I could hardly imagine anyone less suited to being a prep schoolmaster. He clearly found small boys irksome, had no great enthusiasm for teaching and, the ultimate disaster, couldn't keep order. With their built-in antennae, the boys had no doubt discovered this right from the outset and his classes were a shambles.

Part of the problem was that both White's classroom and mine were in a separate wing, well away from those of Blackstone and Hannam. Once, not long after I had started at the school, I heard such a hubbub coming from the next room that I thought that White was absent for some reason. I had never had a moment's problem with discipline myself, probably, I thought, the legacy of having been a prefect at my public school. After a sharp word to the boys in my class, I had no qualms about striding out into the corridor and flinging open the door to the next room.

The sight that met my eyes had me pulling up short in astonishment. The boys had edged their desks forward so that White was hemmed in at the side of the blackboard and they were banging the lids in time as he stared at them with a look of abject terror on his face. I think I can say that I was normally an even-tempered young fellow, but for once I was angry, really angry. I was very close to losing all restraint; the boys knew it and were obviously terrified. I got them all out from behind their desks, lined them up and selecting the most likely ringleader, stared at him from a range of no more than a foot until the boy dropped his eyes and then began to cry.

'Faulkner, you will put all those desks back in position and then you will all sit down and get on quietly with the lesson. There is no excuse for this abominable behaviour and it will not be repeated. Is that understood?'

I put the question to each of them in turn and then left without glancing in White's direction. What I had done proved more effective than if I had issued threats, or reported the class to the headmaster; the word got round and I was looked on with new respect by them all. The big problem, though, as far as I was concerned, I thought afterwards, was White.

Should I ignore what had happened, should I speak to the man, or should I wait for him to say something himself? I would really have liked to have discussed it with someone more experienced like Hannam, but that, I thought, would certainly lead to the episode getting out and would only make life more difficult for the wretched fellow, so I did nothing. White didn't do anything either, not even acknowledging the incident, which mercifully was not repeated, although his classes remained noisy and ill-disciplined. Was the man physically, or even mentally, ill? His shock of black hair accentuated the pallor of his face and he was desperately under-weight, but it was the haunted look, the fact that he was often to be found staring out of the window and jumping at every little noise that was even more disturbing.

It was at the beginning of the summer term during my second year at the school that the atmosphere there began to change. It wasn't anything dramatic, just an accumulation of little things. There was Blackstone himself; whereas before his jokes and actions had always been good humoured, some of them were now malicious. He started to deal out harsh punishments, to use the cane more frequently and was moody, with flashes of bad temper.

There was also Hannam. The man had drunk heavily all the time I had known him — he always put away a couple of glasses of whisky after our games of golf and the level of the brandy bottle also dropped steadily when we played chess, but he seemed to carry it without any difficulty. Now, though, with the war news, particularly in the Far East, being bad, it started to get worse. Although for the most part he was still often urbane and witty, at times, he was morose, touchy and acid-tongued.

One evening, I went down to the lodge to play chess and for once won easily. The reason was not hard to see: the man's voice was slurred; he was quite incapable of concentrating and made a couple of early blunders. With the position hopeless, he resigned and pushed the pieces to one side, looking at me blearily.

'Like another drink?'

'No thanks.'

Hannam refilled his own glass from the decanter, spilling some of the brandy on to the top of the mahogany table.

'Don't you think you've had enough?'

'I don't need cowards who've faked illness

to get out of military service to tell me when I've had enough.'

I flushed and got up to leave, but was pushed back into my chair.

'Maybe that was unfair and if so, I apologize, but you can have no concept of what it was like in 1914-18 when no doubt your head's full of Bulldog Drummond and others of that ilk. It wasn't that fascist oaf with his faithful batman living a charmed life in no man's land and creeping up and breaking a few Krauts' necks with his bare hands before breakfast each morning, nor was it Errol Flynn in immaculate uniform and highly polished boots flying off at dawn to do battle with the Huns, it was day after day and week after week in a stinking trench with your feet half buried in mud, rats scurrying over your face at night and bits of your friends flying around when a shell burst near you. And if you weren't in a trench, you were going over the top and being cut to pieces by barbed wire and machine-gun bullets.

'I may not have a scratch on me, but I have much deeper scars than purely physical ones. Can you wonder that I drink too much, or that it makes me sick having to be dependent on Mr Edward bloody Blackstone with his gung ho philosophy and his fantasies of fighting for God, King and Country? He never had to fight for anything, neither did his father, who made his pile out of armaments manufacture. Oh yes, they were only too happy to employ a war hero — it looked good on the brochure, Captain C.W. Hannam, MC, and all that — but what they didn't know was that I was and still am a gibbering wreck inside, no good for anything except a protected environment like this. I'm almost as bad as David White and that's saying something. Do you know why I spend hours tramping around the grounds almost every night? It's because when I do get off to sleep, I still wake up screaming and it's twenty-five years after it all happened, for God's sake. That's one of the reasons why I live alone and why I still start to dive for cover if a car backfires. Edward's first wife, Helen, was the only one who really understood, but then she died and . . . '

He looked up and suddenly seemed stone cold sober.

'I've no right to ask after what I said to you, but I'd be very grateful if you'd keep all that stuff to yourself.'

'Of course.'

'You'd better go now, Tony. I've said quite enough for one evening, more than enough.'

Neither of us mentioned that evening

again, but after it, the chess contests ceased and even though we still played the odd game of golf, it was always in the company of a couple of the doctors from the local hospital.

I was desperately sorry for the man, but never having encountered a situation remotely like it before, just didn't know what to do and so I took refuge in doing absolutely nothing. What Hannam had said, though, made me look at Blackstone's wife, Barbara, with renewed interest. Up to that time, I had assumed that, young though she looked, she was Patricia's mother, but now the fact that she appeared to have virtually nothing to do with the girl made more sense. She was a shadowy figure as far as I was concerned and she had hardly spoken to me, either, until the day I ran a large wooden splinter under the nail of my forefinger and I went up to the sickbay to consult her.

'I'm afraid this is bound to hurt quite a bit,' she said, when she had looked at it. 'I'll have to cut a wedge out of the nail to get it out and I'm no great expert at this sort of thing. Do say if you'd prefer me to take you down to the local hospital.'

'No, that's all right. You carry on.'

It did hurt, like hell, but she was as gentle as possible and encouraged me by talking to me to help me to take my mind off it and getting me to tell her about my home, my school, my asthma and my time at Cambridge.

'I don't suppose you want to be a prep schoolmaster for the rest of your life?'

'I thought I'd wait to see what opportunities there are when the war's over.'

I flinched as the needle-like pain shot up my hand and arm.

'I was at the Guildhall School of Music and had hopes of becoming a concert pianist, but then the war came and I had to . . . There, got it.' She held up the long splinter in her eyebrow tweezers. 'I do hope that it didn't hurt too much.'

'No, thank you. Not too bad.'

'I'd better put some iodine on it as well.'

After I'd left, I thought about her seriously for the first time. She was a great deal more attractive than I had at first realized, particularly with the twin spots of colour in her cheeks, which had appeared when she had mentioned her music. Why on earth, I thought, had she married Blackstone of all people, who was not only tone deaf, but a good fifteen years older than her, not to mention his having a 12-year-old daughter? I was to wonder that more and more as the months went by.

The arrival of Janet Brice, though, at the

beginning of the winter term of 1944 changed everything.

'Would you like to come down to the pub for a drink?' I asked her, a few days after the beginning of term when she had an evening off.

'I'd love to.'

With my total lack of experience of girls, I had been expecting at best reluctance and, at worst, a refusal, but certainly not wholehearted enthusiasm and a dazzling smile. My first surprise that evening was to discover that she was just as easy to talk to as any of my male friends, the second that we shared much the same sense of humour and finally, that she was as enthusiastic about our first tentative physical contacts as I was.

With anyone older or more sophisticated, I wouldn't have known how to begin, but it seemed the most natural thing in the world to walk back hand in hand, to feel and reciprocate the subtle pressure of her grip and to kiss her goodnight. And what a kiss that had been! There had been so many different sensations, that later that night, when I was in bed and trying to analyse them separately, I was quite unable to do so. There was the velvety texture of her lips, the softness of her body and the way we seemed to fit together. Finally, when I tried to pull away when I felt myself beginning to lose control, she pressed herself even more tightly against me until the explosion was over and then gave me a final gentle kiss.

A visit to the local cinema on our bicycles for our second date may not have sounded very romantic on the face of it, but the back row of the stalls in those days of vigilant parents and restricted opportunities had a very special significance. It was there that we started to make the voyages of discovery that we pursued in the weeks that followed and not the least important part of that for me was to find out that, apart from being every bit as interested and responsive as I was, Janet was a good deal more knowledgeable.

'How on earth did you know about that?' I asked, after she had shown me a variation that I had never even heard of, let alone experienced.

'From reading one of my father's books. I'm fairly strong on the theory, but weak on the practical.'

'If that's what you call weak, I'm not sure I'll be able to cope when you get stronger.'

If she was the one who often initiated new experiments, it was I who discovered the extra frissons of pleasure to be gained by taking risks, which were enhanced by my knowledge that she was frightened of

Blackstone and even more of our being discovered by him during one of our wilder adventures. Our closest call with Blackstone came when he heard us in the bath together and I had to go out of the window, but there was another incident some time later, that spelled the finish of it.

On Sundays, Blackstone, Hannam and I took it in turns to escort the boarders to the local church for morning service. For some reason, probably, I thought, because he would never have managed to keep the crocodile together during the twenty-five-minute walk, White was exempt. That day, it was Blackstone's turn and Janet and I were having a game of ping-pong in the gym, where the table was always set up on Sundays. At least, ping-pong was the game I played, whereas with Janet it was table tennis and no nonsense about it. To make it some sort of contest, I made her play left-handed and to enliven things even further, I got her to agree to a series of forfeits to be undergone by whoever lost each series of five points. Even playing with the wrong hand, she was far too good for me, but after she had won the first three series, setting me some benign forfeits which merely whetted my appetite for what was to come, I at last won one.

'One thing I can't stand, Brice,' I said, in

what I fondly hoped was a passable imitation of Blackstone's rasping voice, 'is when people like you don't try and give of their best. Have you anything to say in your defence?'

She dropped her head. 'No, sir.'

'Well, in that case we'll have to teach you a sharp lesson, won't we? Take down your knickers and bend over the table.'

I held my breath while, with cheeks flushed, Janet stared at me for a moment, than she turned her back, reached up under her skirt and then shuffled across to the table and leaned over it. I took my time, folding her skirt over her back, and after feasting my eyes on her taut backside for a minute or two, took a firm grip on my bat and brought it down with a sharp crack. She gave a jerk, but apart from that didn't move or cry out and I struck again, a lot harder, on the other side. I was just admiring the twin bright pink patches on her white skin when I heard a sharp click from behind me and spun round.

'Quick, Janet, there's someone at the door.'

'Are you sure?' she whispered a few moments later, after she had straightened up and hurriedly adjusted her clothing.

'I definitely heard something. You stay here and I'll take a look.'

The entrance to the gym was by means of two sets of double doors, the inner pair

155

having glass insets and between the two was a small porch. I opened both sets, looked around outside and came back when I saw nobody.

'I'm so sorry, I must have been mistaken.'

She was standing there, cheeks crimson and breathing heavily and I pushed her down gently on to the mat under the wall bars.

'It's all right, I've put the bolts across.'

I had never known her so excited and aroused and when the final moment came, I had to put my hand over her mouth to stifle her cries.

To my relief, when I went back to the main school building, I found that White, who was the only other member of staff to use the common room regularly, wasn't there and I settled into one of the armchairs and tried to make a start on the *Sunday Times* crossword. Half an hour later, though, I had hardly got anywhere, unable to get the events in the gym out of my mind.

'May I have a word with you, Mr Jarrett?'

I hadn't heard anyone come in and nearly jumped out of my skin, then got to my feet when I saw who it was.

'Yes, of course, Mrs Blackstone.'

'What you get up to with Miss Brice in private is, as far as I am concerned, entirely your own affair, but the gym is hardly what I

156

would call 'private'. If anything like that happens again on the school premises, my husband will hear about it and I won't insult your intelligence by underlining what that will lead to. Do I make myself quite clear?'

'Yes, Mrs Blackstone.'

'Good.'

What she had said and the quiet way she had put it was more telling than any lengthy harangue would have been and I made a firm decision not to run any further risks. I saw no reason to tell Janet what had happened and, as it turned out, my resolve was not put to the test. Only a couple of weeks later, Blackstone was found dead and that was the end of it all.

★ ★ ★

'Good God! So Barbara Blackstone must have seen our fun and games in the gym. What on earth must I have looked like?'

'Pink.'

Tony gave me a wicked grin and I burst out laughing. 'Those were the days!'

'They certainly were. She handled it very well all things considered, but it was a bit rich coming from her of all people.'

'How do you mean?'

'She was having it off with White.'

'Are you sure?'

'Absolutely. You remember how cross you were with me after Churchill's broadcast?'

'I certainly do.'

'Well, soon after our little adventure in the gym, when Blackstone was delivering one of his regular Wednesday morning homilies which we all had to attend, I was so bored by listening to him rabbiting on about team spirit and the need for everyone to pull together, that I started to look around. I remember that you were studiously avoiding catching my eye and that Hannam was gazing out of the window, and it was then that I intercepted the look that passed between Barbara Blackstone and David White. Before I met you, I'm quite sure that I wouldn't have noticed it, or at least if I had, wouldn't have realized its significance, but I suppose that with sexual experience had come sexual awareness and I was immediately quite sure that something was going on between the two of them. I became even more certain of it when a day or two later I saw her pick a bit of fluff off the jacket of his suit. It wasn't only that small, intimate gesture, but the smile that went with it that confirmed my belief. You don't think that sounds very convincing, do you?'

'I didn't say a word.'

Tony Jarrett laughed. 'Well, you're quite

right, I didn't think so either, until I more or less discovered them at it.'

'More or less?'

'You may remember that we had something of an Indian summer for a week or two that autumn. It was a Saturday afternoon and Blackstone had gone with the first eleven to an away match, Hannam had taken the rest of them off for a run and I was practising some golf shots on the edge of the games field. I hit a massive slice into the trees and, more in hope than expectation, went in to look for the ball. I was casting around in the undergrowth, when I heard someone moving deep in the wood. I don't know really why I stepped out of sight behind a large tree when I saw that it was Barbara Blackstone — it was most probably nothing more than not wanting to talk to her. She passed quite close to me and you remember how immaculate she always was with not a hair out of place?' I nodded. 'Well, her hair was all mussed up, her blouse was badly creased and in fact she looked a bit like you did after our game of table tennis.

'I was sufficiently intrigued to go through the wood in the direction from which she had come and there, in a small clearing, was a summerhouse. I can't believe that it had originally been sited there — it must have been dumped there when the lawns were converted into the games field. Anyway, I took a look through the window and there, on the floor, with his head on a cushion and partly covered by a blanket, was David White. He was lying flat on his back with his left hand across his face, otherwise, if he was awake, which I wasn't sure about, he would certainly have seen me. I didn't wait to find out whether he was or not and crept away. There was one other curious thing, though.'

'What was that?'

'He had a tattoo on his left forearm. I couldn't make out what it was, but it was quite a narrow band, either in black or dark blue.'

'Good God! It wasn't a series of numbers was it?'

'It might have been. Why do you ask?'

'He was doing dormitory duty for me one night and I found him cowering outside while that big brute of a boy, Fraser, was marching up and down pretending to be Hitler. White was scared out of his wits and it didn't make sense at the time, but it does now.'

'What does?'

'That tattoo must have been his concentration camp number — I had a patient when I first started the practice, who showed me hers.'

'And that would also explain why he never rolled his sleeves up, not even on the hottest day, or when he was going through the motions of bowling in the nets.'

'But how could he possibly have escaped? I've always thought that no one did.'

'I believe that some managed to get out before the war. I don't know the details, but perhaps if enough money changed hands, or there was a relative who had influence in the right places, it might have been possible.'

'It would also explain his accent,' I said. 'Blackstone must surely have known about his being a refugee, but did he know about what the man was up to with his wife and if so, did he perhaps threaten to turn both of them out and was killed as a result?'

'You're going to have your work cut out trying to find out. Why, for that matter, was Hannam cut out of Blackstone's will? Did the two of them have some almighty row and if so, was he the murderer? I felt really sorry for the fellow. What on earth can have become of him with the school closing like that?'

7

Tony Jarrett pressed me to stay longer, but I wasn't even tempted. I hadn't regretted seeing him again for one moment and we had unquestionably spent a memorable evening together, but I wasn't ready for any more serious involvement and I was pretty certain that he wasn't either. Had it been a hint of relief on his face that I had seen when I told him that I had to go? I wouldn't have been in the least surprised if it had; he was comfortably set in his ways and I suspect that for him, as for me, it had been a pleasant diversion and no more than that. I have always had gut feelings about decisions and my mood on the drive back to Chichester was quite enough to tell me that I had made the right one. Apart from that, I also knew that I hadn't lost all my sparkle and zest for life and I felt both alert and quite literally years younger.

When I got home, I stood myself a meal at a new restaurant which had just opened near the cathedral and after an excellent night's sleep, set to work writing up notes on all the information I had gleaned so far. There was

Medley, bullied by Blackstone and who had shown an interest in arsenic; Patricia, profoundly upset by something on the night her father was killed and physically and quite possibly sexually abused by him; Hannam, psychologically damaged in the First War, resenting Blackstone and cut out of his will; and Barbara Blackstone, suspected by her husband of having poisoned him and clearly having had an affair with White, who himself, poor fellow, was obviously unbalanced, probably as the result of his concentration camp experiences.

I still felt uneasy about tackling Patricia and so I wrote to Richard Medley to tell him that I had to go away for a few days and wouldn't have any news for the time being and then I went up to London to see Pamela Wainwright again in her office. There was an aura of quiet competence about the grey-haired woman, who listened carefully to what I had to say while making notes on the pad beside her. I wouldn't have liked to have had her on my trail if I had been guilty of tax evasion; I sensed an iron determination behind her polite and precise manner.

'Let me see now; if this Mr Hannam served in the First War, he would, as you say, be well over a hundred years old by now if still alive and on statistical grounds alone that would be unlikely in the extreme. Why not look up his death certificate as you did with Mr Blackstone?' She took off her glasses and her lips tightened slightly as she looked at me. 'It would save you some expense.'

'That's a good idea, I'll do it on my way home. How about White and Mrs Blackstone? Do you think it's going to be very difficult to find them?'

'I very much doubt it. If, as you suspect, the man had been in a concentration camp, that, combined with his appearance, makes it quite likely that he was Jewish and in that case, he may well have changed his name from Weiss and been in receipt of a pension from the Germans after the war. Various Jewish relief organizations also have excellent records, so I don't anticipate any great problem with him. Mrs Blackstone may not be quite so easy to trace. Let me see now, what have we got to go on? She would be in her very late seventies by now, she studied piano at the Guildhall School of Music and was probably having an affair with White. Anything else?'

'Not that I can think of without asking her stepdaughter and I'd rather not do that at the moment.'

I was considerably shaken by my further visits to The Family Records Centre and the offices of the local newspaper. On Christmas Day, 1944, Colin Hannam had shot himself in the head with his old service revolver. Had it not been for the fact that one Colonel Forbes, a retired army officer, who was walking past the lodge with his dog at the time and recognized the sound of the shot, the body might well have remained undiscovered for some time. The short report in the paper finished with the sentence: *It appears that Mr Hannam had become very depressed after the closure of Brantwood School, which followed the tragic fatal accident which befell his friend, Mr Edward Blackstone, the headmaster.*

Poor Hannam. While it was true that I hadn't known him at all well, he had always been pleasant to me, particularly during the time we were sending the boys back home early. It was on my last night at the school that he took me out to dinner. Before I had gone to Brantwood, it would never have occurred to me to question his motives, but I was no longer the naïve and inexperienced young girl I had been at the start of that term and I was deeply suspicious of them.

I remember that beforehand I had worked out all sorts of stratagems to deal with all the possible ways with which he might have tried to take advantage of me — I like that expression, it makes me think of Gothic horror stories of wicked Sir Jaspers having their way with innocent maidens — but none of them was needed. Indeed, I was quite ashamed of myself when he delivered me back to the school at the safe hour of ten o'clock without giving me a moment's anxiety.

I was full of chat in those days, but even so, on looking back, I can hardly remember a time before or since when I had been so relaxed with a member of the opposite sex — I don't count Frank, or my father, who were special cases. There were no sexual overtones at all and, in particular, nothing like the highly charged relationship I had had with Tony Jarrett, nor was there any feeling of the considerable age gap. It was true that I did, or was encouraged to do, most of the talking, but he seemed genuinely interested in what I had done, my plans for the future and my views on this, that and the other. I don't recall having done so, but I suppose I must have asked him what was going to happen to the school, but if I did, he must have fended the question off, because the first I heard of it closing was when he saw me off in the taxi the following morning. Despite what Tony Jarrett had told me about him, I had never got the impression that Hannam disliked

Blackstone — I had often seen them in deep discussions with one another, which I presumed had been about the management of the school. Clearly, though, there had to be some explanation for the headmaster having cut him completely out of his will. Had the man, then, committed suicide in a fit of remorse after killing Blackstone? I suppose it was possible, but how, in that case, had he managed to be as efficient as he had been in the days that followed the headmaster's death and so charming and endlessly patient with the parents?

I was beginning to feel distinctly depressed about the whole business and I think I might well have decided to give up my enquiries altogether and let sleeping dogs lie had I not received a letter from Pamela Wainwright a week later together with a note of her charges.

Mr David White formerly Weiss, died on 24 October 1982 of a heart attack at the age of 64. He married Barbara Blackstone, née Stanhope, in May 1946. He became one of the interpreters at the Nuremberg trials and later worked for the Overseas Service of the BBC and also for an organization of Nazi hunters. He lost all his family in Dachau. His

widow, Barbara, is now aged eighty-one,
but is still working as a piano teacher.

Also enclosed was a note of the woman's
address and a photograph of an advertisement offering her services as a piano teacher
in the window of a newsagent in Hampstead,
which gave me her telephone number and
stated that she took on both beginners
and more experienced players.

If I did decide to see her, I knew that
I could always stay with my son Paul, but I
really wanted to discuss it all further with
someone else first and I didn't think he would
be the right person. It wasn't that we couldn't
talk — we had, in fact, always enjoyed a
friendly and relaxed relationship — but since
Frank's death, it hadn't been quite the same.
There was a restraint between us, the feeling
that neither of us wanted to upset the other,
which caused him to be more jocular than
usual and me to resent both that and the
advice he tried to give me. No, I knew that he
wouldn't be suitable.

I was jotting down other possible names
such as Tony Jarrett, Richard Medley, my
GP, my solicitor and Pamela Wainwright,
all of whom I rejected for one reason or
another, when I suddenly thought of Alastair
Henderson, the pathologist. He had seemed

interested in the story, he had asked me to let him know how I had got on and he had had forensic experience. He seemed so obviously the best choice that I decided to ring him up there and then.

'How nice to hear from you,' he said, when I had explained that I wanted to talk to him about it all. 'The whole business has been very much on my mind recently, ever since, in fact, I got the report about the arsenic and started to remount those specimens. Any chance of coming to dinner at my club one evening? They do one pretty well there and I know a quiet corner we can use afterwards. Any evening except next Tuesday would suit me — I've got a meeting then.'

'How about the day after tomorrow, or would that be too soon?'

'No, that would be fine for me. Would it be all right if I met you there, say at about seven?'

Fiona, my daughter-in-law, welcomed me with open arms when I explained that I had some things to do in London, particularly as Paul was away for a few days at a meeting of The Thoracic Society, and I wasn't too sorry about that, either. I somehow didn't think that he would have let me get away with the simple statement that I was going out to dinner with a friend. He would have wanted to know with whom and would have wormed the story out of me in minutes.

Alastair Henderson was waiting for me in the impressive hall of the club. He had put on a clean shirt for the occasion, but the collar was frayed and there was something suspiciously like egg on his tie.

'Shall we go straight in? I don't know about you, but I'm starving.'

'I didn't know that women were allowed in places like this,' I said, looking around after we had ordered.

'Oh yes; we wouldn't get away with excluding them these days, now would we? Joking apart, I'm glad to say that we took the necessary steps quite a long time ago and although there were those who thought that the walls would come tumbling down as a result, as you can see, they haven't. People may laugh at London clubs, but this one's been a life-saver for me ever since my wife died. I'm always meeting interesting people here; it's warm and comfortable and has an excellent restaurant. I don't know about you, but as I get older, I get more and more attracted by things that are solid and unchanging, or at least give the illusion of so being. Half of me is aware that there aren't all that many young members and the club's permanence is certainly not guaranteed, but the other half doesn't want to know about things like that.'

He was a thoroughly nice man and throughout dinner kept me entertained with stories of famous trials and murder cases, in some of which he had been involved himself and keeping in touch with the field had remained a hobby after his move into neuropathology.

'Do you know anything about the case of Madeleine Smith?' I asked.

'Yes, I do, as it happens. Why do you ask?'

'I just happened to hear something about it the other day and with arsenic being very much on my mind, it intrigued me. The person relating the story said that the woman poisoned her lover by painting an 'intimate part of her anatomy', as he delicately put it, with arsenic paste and then persuading him to indulge in oral sex.'

'Yes, that was a theory put forward in a book written some time in the middle seventies.'

'Not before that?'

'No. I have studied the case in considerable detail and oral sex was altogether too strong meat for contemporary authors, or indeed those who wrote about it afterwards until really quite recently. The prosecutor, the Lord Advocate, decided not to use the more lurid passages in the woman's letters in the presentation of his case for reasons which he did not explain, although it may well have been that he found them so distasteful that he couldn't bring himself to do so. It may also have had something to do with the fact that if the spicier bits had been read out in court, the press would have had a field day. It was perfectly permissible then to publish material produced in court that would never have been allowed in a book.

'It was an altogether fascinating case. Madeleine Smith had quite openly bought arsenic, even signing for it in the pharmacist's book and saying that she wanted it as a rat poison, but later claimed that she was using it as a cosmetic, a practice current at the time. Her lover, Émile L'Angelier, was also known to be an arsenic taker; he was using it as a stimulant and as an aid to virility. At the postmortem, a massive amount of arsenic was found in his stomach and the big question arose as to how it got there.

'He must have ingested it at most a few hours before his death and it was suggested either that he took it himself as an act of suicide, or that Smith gave it to him in a chocolate or cocoa drink on the night in question. The problem with the latter was that there was no certain evidence that he had visited her that night, L'Angelier was said not to like chocolate drinks and that amount of arsenic would never have dissolved in one cup or a mug. Finally, no trace of either the indigo or soot with which the arsenic that Madeleine Smith had bought had been adulterated, was found in the man's stomach.'

'What about the oral sex theory?'

'The author of that book on Madeleine Smith I mentioned just now, who put forward the theory didn't really give any details. He discussed the rumours circulating at the time and there may have been allusions to it in Smith's letters, but he does not quote any particular passage to prove his point. However, having said that, it does not strike me as being far-fetched; L'Angelier used arsenic as a sexual stimulant and Smith was certainly sexually uninhibited and, for the times, obviously something of an exhibitionist — that is quite clear from her letters. The author was not trying to suggest that all the arsenic was taken in that way, just a proportion of it.

'Anyway, although most commentators over the years have considered that the woman had done it, others have pointed out that L'Angelier was highly unreliable and there have also been suggestions that he was trying to get rid of her. Anyway, the jury wasn't able to make up its mind and a verdict of non-proven was brought in on the main charge of murder by a majority of ten to two.'

'I gather that she married a couple of times, had children and lived to the age of ninety-three in the USA.'

'That's right. The story has all the ingredients of which melodrama is made, including the possibility that she got clean away with murder. It's great stuff and that book is particularly well written. I think you'd enjoy it and I'd be glad to lend it to you, if you like — it's amongst my forensic collection.'

'Would you? I'd be absolutely fascinated to see it, particularly with the arsenic connection.'

'Where are you staying?'

'With my son and daughter-in-law in Kew.'

'I tell you what, I'll take you there at the end of the evening and we could stop at my place in Fulham and pick it up.'

'But Kew's far too far out of your way.'

'Think nothing of it.'

'Why did you give up forensic medicine?'

'Because it's really a job for a young man. Nowadays, getting up in the middle of the night and tramping across muddy fields in wellies to view bodies has long since lost whatever attraction it had for me and there

174

was also the stress of court appearances, which was beginning to get too much for me.'

'I can well understand that. I've only once had that doubtful privilege when I was supporting a patient of mine in a divorce case. I could cheerfully have strangled the judge. Admittedly it was thirty years ago, but he seemed to think that the poor woman should happily have put up with physical and sexual assaults from her husband without complaint.'

'Things have improved a good deal recently, but some of the older ones are still not beyond coming up with the odd asinine comment.'

After dinner, we went into one of the small committee rooms with a pot of coffee and I got out my notebook and went over the whole affair in as much detail as I could.

'Now obviously, if I do decide to pursue it further,' I said, 'I'll have to see Barbara White and Patricia, but my big difficulty is in deciding how accurate Medley, Tony Jarrett's and my memories of all those events are after more than fifty years. That's not the only thing, there's something else that worries me, too.'

'What's that?'

'Leaving Hannam out of it for the moment, Medley, Barbara White and certainly Patricia all had motives for killing Blackstone and would I be justified in stirring things up after all that time?'

'I see what you mean. I reckon that what you really need is another independent account from someone who wasn't emotionally involved with it all and then make up your mind.'

'But how on earth would I set about achieving that?'

'Why not talk to one of the other boys in Medley's form, or his dormitory for that matter?'

'I don't see how . . . Hold on, I've just remembered something.'

I took the Brantwood news sheet out of my bag and spread it out on the table.

'Yes, here it is. 'The Appleby Prize for classics was won by Pedlow, who will be sitting for the Winchester College scholarship next summer.' Medley mentioned Pedlow several times to me — he was just about his only friend at the school apart from Patricia — and I'm absolutely certain that he was in the same dormitory as the two of them. It's also more than likely that they were in the top form together, particularly as he and Medley were going in for scholarships at the same time. Richard Medley managed to find his way into Who's Who and perhaps it's not too much to hope that Pedlow did the same.'

Henderson raised his thumb. 'Good thinking.' He laughed as he saw my raised eyebrows. 'Yes, I know it's a dreadful expression, but in this case it fits the bill admirably. Hang on here and I'll get a copy from the library. Let's hope that the worthy Pedlow's still with us.'

I was looking at the picture of the moon-faced, very plump boy in the school photograph when he came back.

'You've struck oil — I couldn't resist a quick look up there. Here it is. He's a knight, no less, distinguished career in the diplomatic corps, several ambassadorships and now director of Life After Seventy. What on earth's that, do you suppose?'

'No idea, but it's just what I need.'

Henderson laughed. 'That I find difficult to believe. Anyway, the fellow's a member of The Reform Club, which is only a few yards away, and he's given it as his address — no doubt saves him from cranks and all the junk mail. I'll look up Life After Seventy in the register of charities on our way out — that should be the simplest way of flushing him out.'

★ ★ ★

I started the book on Madeleine Smith the following morning and I found it absolutely fascinating, but more than that, it gave me a great deal of food for thought. During one of my breaks from reading, I rang the number of Life After Seventy that Henderson had given me and discovered that it was a charity responsible for the development of leisure activities for that age group, including holidays and outings and that Pedlow was in the USA looking at comparable organizations over there, not being expected back for another few days.

I did hesitate before telephoning Barbara White, but not for long, doing so soon after breakfast the following day. In a way, it was a compulsion — I just had to hear her side of the story and I wasn't prepared to wait until Pedlow returned to London. I didn't succeed in getting through straight away; there was a message on her answer-phone to the effect that she was out and would ring back if I left my name and phone number. She did so half an hour later and we agreed a time for an appointment for a lesson at her house in three days' time, which suited me well as I wanted to finish the book before seeing her.

I went to Hampstead in good time and found her house without difficulty. It was up a narrow and very steep side street within a short walk of the underground station and after I had had a look at it, I went back to the main road for a cup of coffee, deliberately waiting until a couple of minutes before eleven before ringing the bell.

Barbara Blackstone had been pretty, if rather severe looking, as a young woman and now in her old age was both handsome and elegant. She was one of those rare and lucky people to have snow-white hair, which made my dreary grey feel even more dowdy than I already knew it to be, and she had also remained slim and upright.

'Janet Cresswell? Do come in.'

She led the way into the sitting-room on the first floor, where there was a very fine Bechstein.

'You said on the phone that you had played quite a lot when you were at school and wished to take it up again now that you have retired. Have you kept it up at all?'

To get the conversation round to Brant-wood, I had originally intended to admit straight out who I was and to pretend that I was writing a book about my experiences during the war, but suddenly remembered what Miss Fairbank had said to me at school when she had caught me out in a silly lie: 'One lie so easily leads to another and then to endless complications — it's so much simpler in the long run and nearly always better to tell the truth.' And so I faced her fair and square and explained about Richard Medley; how he had asked me to approach Patricia and what had followed on from that.

'And so you think that Edward was murdered?'

'The pathologist didn't seem to have any doubt that not only was he being poisoned with arsenic, but that he was hit on the top of the head by a blunt instrument before falling into the pool.'

Her lips came together and before she could say anything further, I decided to use a technique that had worked for me before when dealing with difficult patients and their relatives. 'Look,' I said, 'I had no business to barge in unannounced on you like this and I'll quite understand if you don't want to talk to me. I've also no doubt taken up teaching time and I'll gladly pay your fee.'

'How did you find me?'

'Through a woman who specializes in tracing people. You're no doubt wondering why I've gone to this trouble?'

She nodded and I explained how depressed I had become after Frank's death and how having something to do after Medley's visit and thinking hard about what had happened at the school had stopped me feeling sorry for myself.

'Yes, I can understand that. As far as David

180

was concerned, it was very painful for him at first, but in the long run he was helped greatly by talking at first to me and then to a psychiatrist about all the terrible things that had happened to him and his family in Germany. It was extremely hard for me, too, and there were times when I could hardly bear to hear about it yet again, but in the end it worked and we were very happy together.

'David never asked me why I had married Edward and I thought it was wrong to burden him with my troubles, which were insignificant compared with his. I still think that was right and in my English way I was suspicious of introspection, so I never sought counselling or help, neither did I unburden myself to a friend. Perhaps that was because I never had the right sort of friend.'

I took one look at the utter sadness on her face and started to get up.

'Please don't go. I would like to talk about it — I think it is about time that I did. I was going to have my hair done this afternoon, but that can wait. I'll give them a ring to put it off.'

I took her out to lunch and afterwards we talked right through the afternoon and into the evening.

8

My piano teacher at school and I were thrilled to bits when I won a place at the Guildhall School of Music, but in my heart of hearts I knew that my father wouldn't let me go and I said as much to Miss Masterton.

'You can't mean it — he let you go up for the interview and audition.'

'That was only because I kept on at him and it was the only way he could think of to shut me up. Anyway, he was expecting me to fail — he said so, often enough.'

'Barbara!' She seemed genuinely shocked. 'You shouldn't speak about your father like that.'

'But that's the way he is. He doesn't believe that women should have a career. According to him, their place is in the home, either looking after a family or their parents. The only reason he let me have piano lessons in the first place was because he considers it a ladylike accomplishment and he thought I would be able to help out at functions in the church hall and on the organ. He never expected me to be any good. He won't let me go, I just know he won't.'

It turned out exactly as I had anticipated. My father had never heard anything so ridiculous in his life. He couldn't afford to support me as a perennial student and London wasn't the place for a young girl, particularly with threats of war in the air. To make it even more pointed, he delivered a sermon the very next Sunday on the ingratitude of modern youth and campaigns for the emancipation of women threatening the very fabric of society.

Even though I had been expecting it, I was bitterly disappointed and the only satisfaction I was able to get out of it was to say I told you so to Miss Masterton, although I didn't, of course, put it quite so baldly as that.

'But you can't give up an opportunity like that. Would it help if I spoke to him?'

I knew that it wouldn't, but it was kind of the woman to offer and if nothing else it would show her that I wasn't exaggerating. When I saw Miss Masterton coming out of his study in tears I suddenly decided that I had had enough of my father's bullying. He bullied me; he bullied my mother, he bullied the parishioners; he even bullied the family cat. I was going to leave home and go up to London and that was the end of it.

I would never have achieved it without help, but an ally was at hand in the shape of my maternal grandfather. He had never approved of his only daughter marrying The Revd Stanhope, who was much older than her and whom he was wont to call 'a psalm-singing fool' when he was particularly irritated by him, which was almost all the time. He had even moved to Grantham after his retirement, much to his son-in-law's annoyance, so that he could be there to support both his daughter and me, his only granddaughter, who was the apple of his eye.

My grandfather, old Bert Grainger, was a bit of a rough diamond — he had made his money in the post-war boom in the building trade — but I loved both him and my grandmother dearly. They were fun, they let me play on their superb Bechstein, which I suspected he had bought specially for me when my father refused to let me practise on the aged upright in our dining-room on the grounds that it interfered with his concentration. I was also able to work there for my higher certificate without being continually interrupted by my father to run errands or laboriously type out one of his sermons.

From time to time, my grandfather was also in the habit of slipping me one of the lovely, large white five-pound notes, which looked so impressive and were a fortune as far as I was concerned, so that I could buy myself clothes and knick-knacks, which my father considered both frivolous and unnecessary. My grandfather would help, I was certain of it, and he did.

'You go,' he said, when I had told him what had happened. 'I ran away from home when I was sixteen and it was the best thing I ever did. I was going to leave you some money anyway, but there's no reason why you shouldn't have part of it now. The income from it should be enough to allow you to live modestly while you're studying.'

With Miss Masterton's assistance, I made all the arrangements, booking a place at the central YWCA in London and then came the day when I faced my father with it.

'What is it now?' he asked irritably, when I knocked on the door of his study and went in. 'Mr Renton is on his way to see me.'

He went white with rage when I told him about my plans.

'You'll do no such thing.'

'Father, I've made up my mind and I'm going next week.'

'You'll come with me up to your room this very moment, I'm going to lock you in and you'll stay there until you see sense.'

'I don't think you understand, Father, I mean it. I'm going up to London and there's nothing you can do to stop me.'

'Oh, so that's what you think, do you, young lady? I tell you what,' he said picking up the long ruler from the top of his desk, 'I'm going to do something to you that I should have done long ago.'

He got up and, as he started towards me, through the window I saw the church warden walking up towards the front door.

'Barbara! What do you think you're doing?' he said, his voice rising in pitch as I took a couple of steps backwards and then began to undo the buttons on my blouse.

'I'm going to take off all my clothes and then I'm going to scream.' It was at that moment that the doorbell rang and I started to ease the garment off my shoulders. 'And that is only a sample of what I'm going to do if you try to stand in my way.'

Would I really have done it if it had come to the crunch? I very much doubt it, but my father wasn't to know that and he went ashen pale and looked away, recoiling from me and I knew that I'd won. My father was a prude and, like many bullies, he was also a coward and, most importantly, at that moment believed that I was quite capable of doing precisely what I had threatened.

'Very well,' he hissed through clenched teeth, 'but you will not go next week, you will go now. I do not expect to see you when I have finished with Mr Renton, nor ever again. You are no daughter of mine. Now, put that blouse back on, you disgust me.'

My grandfather let out a great guffaw of laughter when I told him about it an hour later.

'He really said that? Don't tell me he left out the 'don't darken my door again' bit.' He took me in his arms and gave me a bear hug. 'That was very brave of you, Barbara, and I wish I could have seen his face when you started to undress. That was brilliant. What on earth gave you that idea?'

'My father has an absolute horror of what he calls 'immodesty' in dress — that's one of the reasons he would never go to the seaside or watch me when I was swimming for the school — and as for nudity . . . I forgot to lock the bathroom door once and he came in when I was sitting in the bath. I thought he was going to have a heart attack.'

'I'm not surprised. It was a miracle you were ever conceived — it must have been a very dark night indeed.'

'Bert, whatever will you say next?'

My grandmother was pretending to be shocked, but I could see that she was having a not altogether successful battle with herself, trying not to laugh. Perhaps, I thought, the highly coloured stories I had heard from my

187

school friends about what doing 'it' involved had not been so wide of the mark after all and if so, it was almost impossible to believe that my father could have achieved it. Seeing my obvious embarrassment, my grandmother came up and gave me a kiss.

'There, Bert, you've gone and upset her with your silly jokes. Now, dear, what about your mother?'

I felt the tears beginning to well up. 'She was out, and I didn't wait because I didn't want Father to use her as a lever.'

'You were quite right. Your grandfather will go round and sort things out with her. Don't you worry, this is your home now and your mother can see you here as much as she likes.'

'But what is she going to think? I hadn't even told her what I was going to do.'

'Your mother knows more about the situation than you think — she'll understand.'

My grandmother was right. There were no recriminations, no violent emotional scenes and at the station when my mother saw me off on the train to London, she turned out to be calmer and stronger than I would have believed possible.

'Don't be too hard on your father,' she said. 'You have to remember that he was born and brought up in very different times and has never managed to adapt to all the changes that have occurred since the war. Keep in touch, write to him, let him know how you're getting on and I'm sure he'll come round, I know he will.'

She was wrong. I did try to make allowances, but it was difficult to do so when my grandfather was even older and he hadn't remained stuck in Victorian times with outdated values. I did write regularly to start with, but when I discovered that all my letters had been thrown away unopened, I gave up. In any case, there were far too many exciting things happening in London for me to keep worrying about Father. There was the joy of mixing with so many talented musicians, the new friends I was able to make and the sheer enjoyment of being free.

The outbreak of war at the beginning of my final year didn't even put too much of a damper on things. To start with, rumours abounded and anxiety, verging on hysteria, was in the air, but as the months went by and the bombs didn't start to drop, the routine went on much as before. It was in the golden summer of 1940 that it happened. It had been an emotional time. There was relief, tinged with a sense of anticlimax that the exams were over; the satisfaction of having done really well; the lingering grief at the death of my grandparents within a fortnight of each other only a few weeks earlier. The fact that I had just had my twenty-first birthday and with the money I had been left was well and truly independent. Finally, there had come Dunkirk and the fall of France, which brought with it real fear of bombing and invasion.

One afternoon, I was sitting back on a bench in Regent's Park watching a barrage balloon as it floated white against the blue sky. With such a tranquil scene and the warm sun on my face, I knew that I ought to be feeling relaxed, but I wasn't. I felt unaccountably restless; there was a pulse beating in the pit of my stomach and . . .

'Hot, isn't it?'

I turned my head to see a young man standing by me. As he smiled at me, he ran his fingers over the RAF wings on his jacket, which looked as if they had only been sewn on the previous week.

'It certainly is. Are you on leave?'

'Just for forty-eight hours. We're expecting the balloon to go up at any time now and as I don't know London, I thought I'd do some sightseeing while the going's good, but it's not exactly the weather for it.' He laughed. 'All I've managed to achieve so far is a visit to Madame Tussaud's.'

'That's more than I have, even though I've lived not all that far away for the last three years.'

'Go on.'

'No, it's quite true.'

We went for a stroll together through the rose garden, we hired a boat and went for a row on the lake and held hands while we watched the chimpanzees playing in the zoo. Before, I had always been tongue-tied when talking to strange young men, but this time there was no such difficulty. I told him about my music and my hopes of becoming a soloist when I had studied further and the war was over and he responded with descriptions of the thrill of flying and the comradeship of the squadron.

Why, I was to ask myself so many times over the next few weeks, had I agreed to go back to his hotel room after we had gone out to a night club for dinner and dancing? There were many answers to that question: he was young, good-looking and attractive; I was feeling sexually aroused myself, although at the time I didn't recognize it for what it was, and the unaccustomed alcohol had also had its effect. More than that, though, was the discovery that what he had said about the glamour of flying simply wasn't true. He had seen action over Dunkirk; his best friend had died after receiving terrible burns, and the truth was that he was scared, so scared that at times he was hardly able to climb into his aircraft and couldn't get off to sleep at night. When eventually he did, it was even worse and he would wake sweating and crying out with the recurring nightmare of flames licking around his own cockpit.

I desperately wanted to comfort him and was it so stupid or wicked that I should have given him the one thing that he wanted to experience more than anything else before he was killed? It did cross my mind that he might have put it like that to blackmail me emotionally into agreeing, but that wasn't true, I was quite sure of it. He was absolutely certain that he was going to die and intuitively I realized that that belief was the surest way of making it come true. And so I did comfort him in the way he wanted. He was clumsy and it hurt me, but it wasn't that bad and I managed to conceal it. Anyway it didn't matter when he fell asleep afterwards and I saw how calm and peaceful he was. I got out of the bed, stood there looking at him for a long time and then, my mind made up, dressed and crept out of the room.

When I thought about it, which I did constantly in the days that followed, the whole episode seemed quite unreal. Had I really done 'it' and was that all there was to it? It had been a brief, painful and not in the least enjoyable experience for me and why, in that case, had it seemed so marvellous for him? After it was over, he had burst into tears, thanked me, told me I was wonderful and then he had fallen asleep like a baby. Why hadn't I stayed with him? When I came to analyse it, although I thought I had acted instinctively, I realized that there were a number of reasons behind my decision: I was frightened that he would want to do it again; I didn't want to be pitch-forked into a relationship with, or even marriage to a young man I didn't know at all and there was also the legacy of shame that had rubbed off from my father.

I was almost totally ignorant about sex and what knowledge I did have was a mixture of elementary biological fact, which had been presented at my school by the employment of so many euphemisms, circumlocutions and analogies as to be virtually incomprehensible, and old wives' tales, half truths and rumours culled from friends and reading books, which were passed round at school and which were every bit as misleading. One of the myths that I had come across and believed, was that one couldn't get pregnant by doing it just the once, so when I missed my period and began to get morning sickness, I was absolutely shattered when one of my more worldly friends took me to the Marie Stopes clinic and my worst fears were confirmed.

On my friend Helen's advice, I drank the best part of a bottle of gin, had boiling hot baths and jumped up and down violently for as long as I was able in the hope that something would work, but nothing did. I would probably have been told about the possibility of paying for an illegal instrumental abortion if Helen hadn't left London to seek a teaching post in her home town, but there was no one else to turn to, my whole circle of friends having broken up. What was I going to do? Returning home was out of the question. I couldn't stay alone in London to have the baby and there was no hope of tracing the young RAF pilot, even if he were still alive. The Battle of Britain, as it came to be known, was at its height and I hadn't known anything more about him than that his first name was Tom and that he flew Hurricanes. Would it be possible to go as a companion or housekeeper to some elderly woman who would understand and take me in?

I was half-heartedly flicking through the advertisements at the end of *The Lady*, which I had picked up at the hairdresser, when I saw the advertisement for matron at Brantwood School, the words 'previous experience not essential' catching my eye. I decided that I had to start somewhere and following my letter, was surprised to receive a reply by return and an invitation to attend for an interview. My second surprise was to find that I was being seen by the headmaster on his own.

'Why are you seeking a job as matron when you have a qualification in music?' he asked when he had gone over my curriculum vitae with me.

'Because I'm pregnant.'

Edward Blackstone raised one eyebrow. 'You're nothing if not direct, Miss Stanhope, but I like that. Tell me more. Who is the father?'

I decided that I had nothing to lose by telling him the exact truth and when I had finished explaining why I had left home and couldn't possibly go back, he nodded.

'And when is the baby due?'

'Some time in March.'

He showed me round the school, explained that it was quite small with only sixty-five boys and that rather over half of them were boarders.

'You've never done anything like this before, so do you think you could cope with being matron? The medical side needn't worry you — by and large the boys are a healthy lot and anyway Dr Franklin is always prepared to come whenever necessary — but there's a lot of mothering to do and you would have to cope with the laundry and make sure they wash properly and change their clothes regularly.'

'I don't see why not.'

'And what about giving some piano lessons? Music teaching here is a gap in our curriculum and I've been anxious to fill it for some time.'

'I'd enjoy that very much.'

'There's one last thing. I have an eight year old daughter — my wife died three years ago — and at the moment she's staying with my brother and his wife. She doesn't pose any problems here because during the term she is a full member of the school and sleeps in one of the dormitories, but it's as well you know about her. To be honest, so far I have seen only one other half reasonable applicant for this job and she seemed to find something unnatural about the way I've handled that particular set of circumstances. What's your view?'

'It seems to me to be a very sensible and practical arrangement at her age.'

Blackstone nodded and then looked at me

very directly for what to me was an uncomfortably long time.

'I like you, Miss Stanhope,' he said eventually, 'and I think we would get on very well, but I can't pretend that this pregnancy of yours is exactly ideal. As I said, I have seen no one else suitable and I'm prepared to offer you a term's trial. If that works out well, then we can consider a more permanent arrangement. The salary is modest, but you will get your keep. Any questions?'

'Yes. If you are satisfied with my term's work and I do stay after that, will I be allowed to keep the baby with me here?'

'Most certainly, but I think it would be in everybody's interests if you were to wear a wedding ring and assume the mantle of widowhood — in a sense, it could be said that you are one. It's not that I personally take a narrow-minded view of such things, but I very much doubt if some of the parents would approve of an unmarried mother as matron. I will not press you for a decision now, but I would appreciate one as soon as possible — term starts next week.'

I didn't need time to make up my mind, indeed I could hardly believe my luck, particularly when the term got under way. To my surprise, I enjoyed the work of matron, I had plenty of time in which to practise the piano and was even able to have a weekly lesson in Chichester with a distinguished teacher, with whom the Guildhall School had put me in touch and who had moved from London to escape the bombing, which had just started in earnest. I also enjoyed my own piano-teaching duties and playing for the community singing that Blackstone was so keen on, despite the fact that he was tone deaf himself.

I liked Blackstone. He was full of energy and bounce and was particularly kind when, not long before the end of term, the baby stopped moving and after several visits to the hospital, I was informed that it was dead. Many people would have told me that it was all for the best, but even though he may have thought so, never once did he say it and was a constant source of comfort and encouragement when I had to endure the long and depressing time while I was waiting for it to be born, which the doctors said was safer for me than having an operation.

I had been at the school for eighteen months when Blackstone asked me to marry him. I didn't even have to work out the pros and cons, he did that for me himself, putting the cons first. He was nearly twenty years older than me; he had had epilepsy in the past, but that was now under control; there was Patricia and he did understand that I might not love him. On the other hand, we got on very well, he would appoint an under-matron, which would allow me time to concentrate on the piano, and after the war, there was no reason why my career shouldn't take off.

I did agonize long and hard about it. It was true that I didn't love the man, but he was fun. I knew he was lonely and it would mean that the future would be secure. On top of that, I owed him so much. One of my major reservations was Patricia. It wasn't that the girl behaved badly or was rude to me — she just treated me in exactly the same way as did the boys, politely but distantly. Blackstone had told me that he had sounded out Patricia before asking me to marry him and that she had seemed happy about it, but if she was, she clearly wasn't in any hurry to show it. How would I be able to cope with a girl, who was now ten and whose sole interests seemed to be in sport and who liked nothing better on a cold winter's afternoon than to go for a run with her father? And how much worse would it be when she reached adolescence?

I still kept in touch with my mother and went to see her during the school holidays, but she wasn't able to help; she was too busy looking after my father, who had had to retire from his ministry, and was showing the signs of Alzheimer's disease, which was to kill him a few years later. In the end, I did agree to marry Blackstone, largely because I couldn't think of any really compelling reason why I shouldn't. To my surprise, the sex side, which I was expecting to have to tolerate as part of the bargain, was hugely enjoyable. To start with, he was gentle and sensitive to my complete lack of experience, but then, as with his classes in school, he proved an enthusiastic and inventive teacher. I was happier than at any other time in my life and my only regret was that I still hadn't managed to make any progress with Patricia.

It started very gradually, so gradually that it took me a long time to realize the full extent of the change that was occurring in my husband. Ever since I had known him, he had been a devotee of patent medicines and health foods and was in the habit of sprinkling garlic over his food. Now, he started to take vitamin supplements as well. His initially polite requests for me to do this and that for him became orders, and his eccentricities, which to begin with I had found endearing, were now often barbed and cruel. He started to take Patricia on climbing and walking holidays, leaving me behind and sexually, he had become demanding and aggressive. After he had forced me to submit to something I had found both painful and degrading, I rebelled. I had finally managed to defeat my father by tackling him head on and I did exactly the same with my husband, the following morning when I went to see him in his study.

'What you did last night, Edward, is something I'm not prepared to tolerate. It was sick, perverted and unnatural and you ought to be ashamed of yourself.'

'You believe that, do you, Barbara?'

'I would have thought that I had made myself perfectly clear.'

'You have indeed. From what you have told me about your father, he was a prude and you appear to have inherited the same characteristic. What you object to has been practised by men and women in every country in every continent for the last several thousand years. Not having had the benefits of a classical education, you may not know that the *hetairai*, who were women in one of the most, if not the most, civilized societies ever, the Grecian, used it through choice as a method of contraception. However, be assured that I have no wish to offend your delicate sensibilities as you will soon discover. Now, if you will excuse me, I have a class to take.'

I left the study puzzled and uneasy, but I soon discovered what he had meant. When I went up to our bedroom to change for supper, I found that he had moved all my things out to a bedroom down the corridor. He treated me with studied politeness both in public and private and we still had our evening meal together alone while the rest of the staff ate separately, but the only things we ever discussed were the war, school matters and his health, with which he seemed to be becoming increasingly preoccupied. He was always trying some new herbal remedy or other and reading out extracts from magazines, which extolled the virtues of various régimes designed to increase vitality.

I felt myself becoming more and more isolated, particularly during the school holidays. My husband always took Patricia away with him and I was left with the Staceys and David White, who like me seemed to have nowhere else to go. Right from the start, I had had very little contact with the other members of staff, something which became more pronounced with Edward's increasingly touchy and difficult behaviour, and this was even more true of White than the others, who were at least prepared to pass the time of day with me. I took to spending longer and longer hours at the piano, particularly out of term and it was during the summer of 1944 that it happened.

Following the death of Rachmaninov the previous year, my teacher, a Russian emigré himself, had encouraged me to study the preludes and I had just finished the one in G minor and was sitting in front of the piano near to tears, when I sensed someone behind me. I turned and saw White standing at the open door.

'That was very beautiful. I love hearing you play.'

It was only very gradually that our relationship developed. White started to sit and listen with rapt attention while I practised; we went for walks together, being careful to avoid being seen by the Staceys, and little by little I learned of the terrible things that had happened to him and his family. I had heard rumours about concentration camps, but had thought that a lot of it was propaganda like tales of Hitler foaming at the mouth and eating carpets, a rumour out of which my husband was fond of making capital. Now, faced with the full horror of the terrible things that David had witnessed, the beatings, the starvation and the inhuman conditions, I was both deeply shocked and ashamed, ashamed because I had been dwelling on the hard times I had had, which paled into insignificance beside those of David White.

'How did you manage to get out?' I asked him one day.

'It was Blackstone's father who made it possible. He had made a fortune out of armaments in the First War and, after the depression in the early thirties, his Jewish business associates told him what was happening in Germany. Typically, he didn't take it on trust and went to see for himself. It's a pity that you never knew Henry Blackstone — he was a remarkable man. My father, who had been a well-known physician in Munich, had been arrested with all the family not long before and Blackstone heard the story from a prominent industrialist, who had been a patient and later a friend of his. Despite his brother being a prominent member of the Nazi Party, the industrialist didn't approve of what they were doing. Using a combination of his influence and Blackstone's money, he managed to get me and a number of other young people out of Dachau. At that time, it was 1938, some Jewish children were being brought over here and even though none of the others was more than fifteen years old, I managed to pass as that, having lost a lot of weight. Although both men tried as hard as they could, sadly they were unable to do anything about the adult members of my family.

'Blackstone senior took a liking to me, brought me here and when my English became good enough, gave me a job. I'm a hopeless schoolmaster and Edward knows it, but his father made him promise to keep me here as long as I wanted to stay and when the man died, Edward kept his word, although I know very well what he thinks of me. He knows that I'm unable to keep order and he also considers that I'm a feeble wreck of a man who can't forget the past and get on with his life and he's right. Many's the time I've wished that Henry Blackstone had left me where I was.'

'Don't say that.'

'But you don't understand the guilt that is constantly with me, but how can I expect you to, when I don't really understand it myself? I know perfectly well that it's sterile and useless to wonder constantly why I should have survived when so many better and more worthy people died, but I can't help it and it's still with me all the time.'

Talking about it all for the first time, and doing so endlessly in the weeks that followed, was probably the start of his eventually being able to come to terms with the past, but at that time reliving the nightmares had a

205

devastating effect on him. He became jumpy and fearful, depressed and tearful and in my desperate attempts to comfort him, the inevitable happened. After all, I was still young and my early experiences with Edward had unleashed my previously suppressed libido. It seemed to help, me as much as him, but once we had started there was no stopping and my constant fear was that my husband would find out, particularly as he had been becoming progressively more paranoid and suspicious, even accusing me of poisoning him. He was also beginning to look unwell, but according to Dr Franklin, too large a dose of his anticonvulsant drugs, particularly the bromides, was responsible for that problem and he arranged for him to be seen by his specialist.

Janet Brice's arrival was a help in many ways, but in others it made it worse, particularly when I began to become progressively more envious of her.

★   ★   ★

'You were envious of me?'
'I'm afraid so.'
'Whatever for?'
'You were such a happy person, looked so fit and were full of bounce with your whole

future mapped out; you seemed not to have a care in the world and, worst of all, you had obviously succeeded with Patricia where I had failed so miserably. I was also envious of your relationship with Jarrett; it seemed so carefree, uncomplicated and even innocent, compared with the hopeless mess I had made in that direction myself.'

'It wasn't all that innocent, I'm afraid.'

'Maybe not, but I knew somehow that you were not the sort either to get pregnant or emotionally entangled with anyone before you were ready.'

'What do you remember about the night of your husband's death?'

'I suppose you think that I killed him either on my own, or with David's help?'

'As it happens, I don't, but I'm sorry, I shouldn't have put it like that; I must have sounded like a bullying police officer.'

'Don't apologize. I wouldn't blame you if you had thought so, but neither of us had anything to do with it. David had got so that he was unable to sleep without me beside him and he was with me in my room all that night. Why do I remember it so clearly? It was because Colin Hannam knocked on the door to tell me that Edward was dead and David very nearly gave us away by crying out — he thought it was the SS coming to arrest him.'

'What about Hannam?'

'Poor Colin. I liked him and although it became quite clear that he retained a special affection for Helen, Edward's first wife, he was always nice to me.'

'Why do you think your husband cut him out of his will completely?'

'I don't know, but it may have had something to do with the row they had only a week or two before Edward's death.'

'What was that about?'

'Edward wouldn't go into any detail, just that Colin had let him down and that he would have to go at the end of term. He said that if he went quietly and without any fuss, which he thought he would, then that would be the end of the matter. I did try to press him further, but that's all he would say. Soon after we got married, Edward gave me a rough idea of his intentions with regard to a new will, but I had no idea that he had changed its provisions until I was told by his solicitor soon after his funeral. I can only presume that Edward's death and then discovering that he had been cut out of the will must have been too much for Colin to cope with.'

'Do you think that Hannam might have killed your husband?'

'It's impossible to say without knowing

what the row was about and what went on between them, but I think it most unlikely. Colin had an absolute horror of violence and was a quiet, gentle person, not in the least pugnacious or aggressive like Edward, even when he drank too much, which I'm afraid he did, particularly during that last term. Edward used to go on about it, so perhaps that had something to do with his decision to get rid of him.'

'Do you think it possible that your husband was bisexual?'

'Good Lord, no. Whatever makes you think that?'

'It just occurred to me that there might have been something going on between him and Hannam, and then there was that thing that he made you do.'

It wasn't only that, I was also thinking about the way Blackstone had brought up Patricia, virtually as a schoolboy, and what she told me when she started her period, which had made me suspect that her father might have abused her in that very way. I had no intention, though, even of hinting of such a thing to Barbara White. In fact, I was worried that I might have said too much already.

'Although I didn't believe what Edward told me at the time,' she said, 'I later discovered that what he'd said was quite correct. I'm sure I don't need to tell a doctor that lots of heterosexual men like that particular variation from time to time and a surprising number of women as well. If I had been aware of that and if Edward had approached it more delicately, perhaps I wouldn't have made such a fuss. Thinking about it now, I did adopt a pretty sickening 'holier than thou' attitude and, all things considered, it's a surprise that Edward didn't react much more violently than he did. No, I don't believe that Edward was a homosexual — I often heard him on the subject of how wicked that was and I'm quite sure that he wasn't putting on an act.'

'You don't think he was protesting too much?'

'No, I don't and, as there were a lot of homosexuals at the Guildhall, with many of whom I was very friendly, I had got pretty good at recognizing them.'

'But your husband and Hannam were originally on good terms?'

'Oh, yes. They shared an interest in football and I remember them going on and on about Brantwood's famous victory against Ravenscourt; they were like a couple of small boys together over it.'

'What happened to Patricia?'

210

'As you no doubt remember, she was whisked off by her uncle and that was the last I heard of her until today. I know it must sound callous to say that it was a relief for me not to have to worry about her, but we had never developed any sort of close relationship and I knew she would be well looked after. I liked what little I had seen of Edward's brother and sister-in-law and I was far too preoccupied with trying to get David well and planning our future to give her any more thought.

'In fact, everything turned out as well for us as I could have hoped. With the money I had inherited both from my grandfather and Edward, I had enough to tide us over and to pay for a psychiatrist for David. The breakthrough came when he was persuaded to act as an interpreter at the Nuremberg trials, which helped to restore his self respect. Afterwards he got a job with the overseas service of the BBC. David and I were so happy together until he died just under twenty years ago and although I still miss him dreadfully, I am content enough with my musical friends and my piano. I did manage to continue my studies; I had a modestly successful career, not as a soloist, but as an accompanist, in chamber music and finally as a teacher.'

'I'm so glad.'

'Do you plan to see Patricia?'

'I'm not sure. There's a lot to think about.'

'If you do, you will let me know how she got on, won't you? I was a rotten stepmother to her and I still feel guilty about it.'

'Of course.'

9

Sir David Pedlow, whom I had arranged to meet in his office, had been a fair, round-faced, tubby small boy and he was much the same now, although he had grown into a very large man indeed. If I had seen him for the first time across the room, say at a cocktail party, I might easily have written him off as a 'silly ass' type, all veneer and nothing much between the ears. He had one of those open, pink faces and was wearing a slightly loud tweed suit, the sort which would have had Jeeves hatching a plot with a view to sending it to Oxfam, if that admirable organization had existed in those days, and I was expecting to hear one of those bleating, upper crust voices to complete the picture. However, the eyes behind the searching look he gave me and the confident, deep, neutrally-accented voice, together with his impressive record, made me think that in his time he must have caused many people, a great deal more clever than me, to underestimate him.

'So, Janet Brice, or should I say Cresswell?' he said, holding out his hand. 'How fascinating to meet you again after all this time, not that I would have known your name if you hadn't explained who you were. You were always 'Matron' to me. And so you were in medical practice with your husband and in your retirement planning to write a book about your own school and Brantwood during the war? Good for you! How can I help you?'

'I've been recalling my own experiences at Brantwood, but I was only there for one term and I was an outsider really; that's why I would like the view of somebody who was on the receiving end.'

'You make it sound like a prison sentence, which, in a way, I suppose it was. How did you find me?'

I had spent a long time thinking about the best way to make an approach to Pedlow and finally decided to say nothing about my suspicions concerning Blackstone's death. However, I felt unless I admitted to having seen Richard Medley, it would make moving the discussion in the way I wanted almost impossible. Why didn't I mention all the others I had spoken to? I'm not sure. It was probably for no other reason than the wish to get a new and unbiased view of Brantwood without any of the overtones that had coloured the recollections of all those I had seen.

'Mr Hannam gave me the school photograph as a memento just before I left and filled in all the names for me. I also remembered that both you and Richard Medley were scholarship boys and guessed that one or other of you or both might have an entry in *Who's Who*.'

'Have you seen Medley already?'

'Yes.'

I told Pedlow the bare bones of the man's career and what a miserable time he appeared to have had at the school.

'That I can well imagine, but it wasn't all bad, you know. It would be fun to have a chat about it. Why not come to my club some time — we're far too likely to be disturbed here and anyway, I ought not to use this office for personal matters — bad for my image.'

The man chuckled, setting his double chins wobbling.

'I'd love to. It's the Reform, isn't it?'

'You have done your homework. The dreaded *Who's Who* again?'

'That's right.'

Pedlow pulled out an expensive-looking, leather-bound diary.

'You're not free this evening are you, by any chance? I spend a good deal of my time attending various dinners and other evening functions and the next week or two are chock-a-block.'

'That would suit me very well if you're quite sure; I wouldn't want to take up your one free evening.'

'Don't worry about that — it would make a nice change from the usual dreary round.'

Two dinners at London clubs within a fortnight! Frank and Paul would have been astonished and so, for that matter, would I have been a year earlier. Even after that modest experience, I was undoubtedly getting a taste for them; they were quiet, the staff were courteous and efficient, the wines were good and the cuisine excellent and where else could you walk down the same staircase as Talleyrand had done after your meal.

'Fire away,' Pedlow said, after we had settled down to coffee and liqueurs. 'What are you particularly interested in?'

'Your impressions of the school as a whole and the people, particularly the staff and the boys in your dormitory, whom I knew the best. As I said, I was only there for one term and your group must have been at the school for a good five or six years by then.'

'Yes, we had. I was six when I first went to Brantwood and I suppose having had two older brothers at the school, one of whom was still there, should have been an advantage, but I'm not sure that it was. Rob, who was the middle one of we three, was a tough small boy, whereas I was a crybaby, and I must have been a terrible embarrassment to him. I must say, though, that he was pretty good about it and did his best to look after me until he left when I was nine or ten. What are my main memories and what was it like? A bit like life, I suppose one might say; there was a lot of fun — I remember the swimming pool in summer and those wonderful film shows — but there was also abject misery in the shape of chilblains that were so bad that my fingers split open, chapped knees chafed by those shorts that we had to wear however cold the weather, and football. If I hated football, then I was absolutely petrified by boxing. I have always been fat, slow, uncoordinated and a physical coward, so you can imagine what it was like. The gloves were heavy and well padded, so there was no real risk of being hurt badly, but I always ended up in tears except the times I used to fight Medley. We were well matched; he was as blind as a bat without his glasses and neither of us had the least desire either to hit or be hit by the other. I remember we just circled around, flailing totally ineffectually at the air.

'Curiously enough, what I enjoyed more

than anything was the academic work and that was largely thanks to that remarkable character Edward Blackstone, who was a great teacher. He may not have been much of a classical scholar, but he certainly made the subject live. Can you imagine anyone being able to inspire a small boy with a love for Latin and Greek verse that stays with him to this day? Well, he did. He had visited the classical sites; he had lantern slides to illustrate them and he had tales of gods, wars, soldiers and slaves. It wasn't dull stuff about Caesar crossing rivers, but what it was like to row in a trireme, to face wild beasts in the Coliseum and to take part in the Olympic games. He probably made most of it up, but by God it was exciting! All right, so I had a natural flair for the classics, but without him I would never have got so enthusiastic about it.

'I was extremely lucky, too, in that my gift in that direction insulated me to a large extent from Blackstone's excesses. If you had drawn up a list of the attributes that he disliked most in small boys, I fulfilled all of them, with the sole exception of class work. I was fat, physically lazy, disliked games of any sort intensely and lacked physical courage. The man was in fact quite mad, almost certifiable in some ways. I don't suppose you

218

were ever told about his crockery smashing phase?'

'No, I wasn't.'

'It was before the war, not long after I first went to Brantwood. He got it into his head that we were full of unhealthy tensions and that the best way to relieve them was to smash plates. He went round to jumble sales buying up old and cracked stock and we had to go one by one into a room he had set aside and set to work with an old cricket stump. He also invented a bowling machine based on the principle of a Roman catapult. It was wonderful and almost converted me to cricket; the very first time he used it, the ball went sailing out of the ground and smashed through Stacey's greenhouse.'

'He seemed to me to be getting steadily more peculiar throughout that last term,' I said.

'He was a funny mixture. On some occasions he could be absolutely terrifying, like the time he beat Patricia, but at others he could behave with surprising sensitivity.'

'Can you give me an example?'

'Well, I don't know whether or not you remember, but Hannam, the deputy head, used to take some of the more senior boys down to the lodge on Sunday evenings for play readings. Afterwards, we had sandwiches and ginger beer. It was one of the highlights of the week. During the time I went, it became more and more elaborate and he started to get us to dress up to make it more life-like — he had the most amazing collection of clothes and wigs in several large trunks.

'It all boiled over when, during that final term we went down early to dress for a performance of *Robin Hood* that Hannam had written specially for us. Patricia was Robin, Medley, Will Scarlet, Fraser, Sir Guy of Gisborne and needless to say, I was Friar Tuck. Do you remember Watson, by any chance?'

'Yes, wasn't he a fair, small boy in the bed by the window?'

'That's the fellow. He was a very pretty boy and Hannan cast him as Maid Marian. Even at the age I was then, I knew perfectly well that it was hardly necessary for Hannam to get Watson to strip off completely while he was making up his face, nor for him to make the wretched fellow put on female underwear, nor for him to have taken so many photographs of it all. There's no doubt that he would have liked to do the same with Patricia, but she wasn't having any of it and I can't say I am surprised — it hadn't escaped my notice that she had been becoming quite a young woman during that term.

'Anyway, with the elaborate wig of flowing locks, Watson looked very fetching and Patricia suitably tough and virile as Robin, while Fraser, with a fierce moustache, was the very personification of evil — he really was a vile boy. I don't know how Blackstone got in, or how long he had been there, he just suddenly put in an appearance while we were removing the make-up afterwards and when the wretched Watson was once more in a state of nature.'

'What did Blackstone do?'

'He was remarkably restrained, considering he had such a thing about homosexuality. According to my brothers, he used to harangue the leavers individually at the end of their last term about the dangers of unnatural practices at public school and he didn't mince words, either. On that occasion, though, all he did was tell us that it was getting late and that we must eat up our sandwiches quickly and he then sent us back up to the school. Nothing was ever said to us about it afterwards, but the scheduled play reading on the following Sunday was cancelled, Hannam never mentioned the subject again and then Blackstone died and we all left anyway.'

'Do you suppose that Patricia reported

Hannam to her father?'

'I think that very unlikely. We all trusted her absolutely not to breathe a word to him of anything that went on at the school and I'm quite sure that Blackstone himself accepted that it would be quite wrong to expect her ever to do so; he had very definite ideas about what was honourable, something he was always going on about it. Anyway, I doubt if Hannam ever did anything more than have a good look, pat the odd passing bare bottom and wrap those getting cold in a large towel and give them a rub, which he liked to do when he was supervising swimming at the poolside during the summer term. Communal baths and showers weren't at all uncommon in private schools in those days and so swimming in the nude with those places that had pools wasn't all that out of the way, either. No doubt you remember the morning cold bath routine?'

'I certainly do and the fact that Patricia was excused it.'

'Yes, but that was only during that last term, when she was obviously growing up.'

'You don't mean that she also swam in the nude?'

'Yes, most certainly she did. She was easily the best swimmer at the school and the only one with enough courage to dive off the top board, with the exception of Blackstone himself, of course.'

'Surely he wore a costume?'

'Good Lord, no. You must remember that in the thirties there was something of a cult of going back to nature and nude bathing was common in scout gatherings, not to mention the Hitler Youth Movement, which, in its early days, was much admired by many in this country. It certainly didn't bother any of us boys, nor Patricia for that matter — it was just a normal school activity. I'm quite sure that there was nothing sexual in it as far as Blackstone was concerned, but, as I said, the same couldn't have been said about Hannam. I'm equally certain that I wouldn't even have given it a second thought had I not been warned to watch out for him by my brother. Once I was on the lookout for it, though, it was as clear as daylight and that he had his particular favourites, like Watson.'

'And was Patricia one of them?'

'Very much so. He liked to look up at her when she was standing on the high board and I also remember his going up on to it himself and helping her to maintain a handstand when he was teaching her to dive from that position. I think Hannam was probably just a bit of a paedophile rather than just a homosexual with a liking for small boys.'

'And Blackstone didn't go in for any of that sort of thing, himself?'

'No, he didn't. With him it was all regimentation and teaching us all to swim with no high-jinks at all.'

'Did you know that Hannam committed suicide on Christmas day that year?'

'Good Lord! No, I didn't. I suppose Blackstone must have decided to sack him, or something, but in that case, why did Hannam kill himself at that particular time? After all, it would have been some weeks after that play of his and not even all that close to Blackstone's death.'

'I think it may have been because he knew that the school was going to close and he felt he had a responsibility to see it through to the end. I saw quite a lot of him when we were packing you all off home and he struck me as being a very lonely and sad figure. He took me out to dinner on my last night and to think that I was worried that he might make a pass at me! In fact, he was extremely nice and we had a most relaxed evening. It never occurred to me then that he might be thinking of taking his own life, but later on in my practice I learned that not only is it very difficult to tell if people are near the end of their tether, but also that Christmas is a time when depressives are particularly vulnerable,

224

especially if they are on their own.'

'Poor Hannam. Kinky he may have been, but he was a very good sort.'

'He taught maths and chemistry, didn't he?'

'That's right, and in the same way that Blackstone liked me because I was good at classics, Medley, with his real gift for maths, was a special favourite of his. I was fascinated to hear what had become of Medley; he was a horrid boy in some ways and even though we were thrown together because we both hated games and were the same age, I never really liked him. He was clever, though, and a remarkable chess player. I used to play him a lot and although I turned out to be one of the better boys at it at Winchester, I never once beat him — my greatest triumph was to achieve one draw by means of perpetual check.'

'There is no doubt that he was absolutely terrified of Blackstone; he even told me that he had thought of poisoning him with arsenic.'

Pedlow laughed. 'That sounds like a bit of typical Medley fantasy — he lived in a world of make-believe. He always had his nose buried in some book or other and one week he would be Richard Hannay, the next Bulldog Drummond and the next Alan Quartermain. I bet he got that arsenic idea from the book on notable British trials that was in the library — it was a special favourite of his and he was always poring over it. He was the sort of boy who was always reading Ripley's *Believe It or Not*, Whittaker's Almanac and, of all things, Wisden. For a boy who detested games, it was ironic that he knew much more about the rules and statistics of cricket even than Blackstone, who was fanatically keen on it himself. Medley was always correcting people with some extraordinary fact or other and what infuriated people was that he was almost invariably right. I think that was the thing that irritated Blackstone more than anything — the man was a great one for the broad brush and dramatic story and had little time for tiresome detail, so I'm sure you can imagine how annoyed he used to get when Medley's hand would shoot up and in that wheedling voice of his would pipe up: 'Please, sir, I read in the *Encyclopaedia Britannica* the other day that . . . ' I felt like kicking him myself often enough.'

'Medley made quite a lot of it to me. He said that there was a bottle of arsenic in the chemistry cupboard in Hannam's classroom and that he had seriously thought of putting some in the salt that Blackstone used to put on his porridge.'

'Sorry to spoil a good story, but that couldn't possibly be true. There were hardly any chemicals in that cupboard and certainly nothing poisonous; there were just a few simple compounds and solvents to demonstrate precipitation and distillation. The chemistry teaching was quite rudimentary.'

'And Hannam didn't tell you about Madeleine Smith and the death of her lover by poisoning?'

'Naturally I can't remember Hannam's stories in any detail, but it seems wildly unlikely to me; the man had an absolute thing about violence of any sort, particularly anything to do with war. I remember once on Armistice Day how upset he got about the phrase 'the glorious dead'; 'there's nothing glorious about death in battle at all', he said, 'it's an obscenity'. It would have been completely out of character for him to have told us about a murder. My God, all this takes me back. I have many fond memories of that place, but some not so fond as well.'

'Such as?'

'I've already mentioned football and boxing, but there was also bullying. Blackstone was a bully: he bullied Medley; he bullied the wretched White and he bullied Patricia.'

'But not you?'

'No, Fraser took responsibility for that in my case. I hated and feared that brutish lout, but not as much as he feared Patricia. It was a most strange thing, he never seemed to learn; he would go on provoking her until he went too far and then it was wham, bam and certainly not thank you ma'am. She was incredibly tough, that girl, and seemed almost immune to pain. I saw the results of some pretty fair old beatings at Winchester, but never anything there remotely like the state her backside was in when her father had finished with her after he caught her cheating in an exam. She didn't so much as let out a peep while he was at it. Did you hear about it at the time?'

'I certainly did and saw the evidence. Do you think that Hannam knew about the way she was treated by her father?'

'Impossible to say for certain, but I imagine so. The boys used to chat to him a lot, which was hardly surprising as he was such a sympathetic person in contrast to Blackstone and, even more so, his wife.'

'Was Patricia a bully, too?'

'Not in the least. Although she didn't appear to have a thought in her head apart from games, she was an exceptionally nice child in many ways. She was always cheerful and quite remarkably loyal, both to us and her father; I never once heard her gossip about him and I'm equally sure that nothing we did ever went back to him. In fact, I was very grateful to her. Robin Hood was a good part for her; she certainly protected the peasantry in the shape of me and Medley from the vicious Guy of Gisborne. She admired you, too.'

'Go on!'

'It's true. I remember it particularly because what she said to me struck me as being so out of character. She had never showed the least interest in her appearance before, but one day, near the end of that last term, when we were washing our hands after she had spilled some ink and I had helped her to clean up the mess, she said: 'Don't you think Miss Brice is pretty?'' Pedlow gave me a smile. 'Naturally I agreed and she looked at herself in the mirror above the basin. 'She's got such lovely hair and one day I'm going to grow mine like that and wear beautiful clothes'. I had a teenage sister at home and was not unfamiliar with the interests and longings of girls of that age, but, do you know, I'm quite sure that that was the first time I ever thought of Patricia as a girl. Sad, wasn't it? Poor little thing; I can understand Blackstone having her at Brantwood when she was small, but at the age of nearly thirteen was quite another matter. Do you know what happened to her? She just seemed to disappear and with all the excitement at the time, I'm sorry to say I never gave her a thought.'

'Her uncle took her away on the day of her father's death.'

'I do hope things turned out all right for her; she certainly wouldn't have got much help from that curious stepmother of hers.'

'I never really got to know her.'

'Neither did we. She was matron for a year or two and had a certain glamour as a war widow, but I was only eight then and was looking for a mother substitute, which I didn't find in her. It didn't make much of an impact on us, either, when she married Blackstone, except that she fairly soon gave up being matron and then you arrived on the scene. I did have a few piano lessons from her, but it soon became clear that the piano and I were not compatible and I persuaded my parents to let me give it up. I must say, though, that for someone who looked like a wet weekend for most of the time, she was remarkably patient with me over that.'

'How about the rest of the staff?'

'Well, I liked Jarrett. He was like a breath of fresh air after the senile old fool who preceded him, whose name I can't even remember. Jarrett had a splendid old HMV wind-up gramophone, one of those with the picture of the dog inside the lid, and fibre needles, which we used to sharpen for him with a special instrument. Let me see, what records used he to play? Ah, yes, one of my favourites was Maurice Chevalier with that delicious accent of his, which we all tried to imitate:

'Ev'ry little breeze, seems to whisper Louise, Birds in the trees seem to twitter Louise, Each little rose tells me it knows I love you, Louise.'

'I can't remember any more except the last line:

'Can it be true someone like you could love me, Louise?'

'And then there was the laughing policemen, a man imitating railway engines, George Formby and some of the wartime favourites like Vera Lynn. He also introduced me to Glenn Miller, whom I've liked ever since.
'His English lessons were always good value, too. He set us interesting subjects on which to write essays, was always prepared to

231

make constructive comments about our efforts and introduced us cleverly and gently to the classics. Like Blackstone and Hannam in their different ways, he also knew how to keep order, which is more than can be said of White, who was pathetic.'

'He always seemed a very sad figure to me.'

'I don't know about that, but he was certainly a disaster as far as my French was concerned and, being a sickeningly law-abiding small boy, I was in a constant state of anxiety about the hubbub in his classes, being terrified that Blackstone might come in. He did, once, when I was about ten and there was a spectacular row, which had me shaking for hours afterwards. The Head came storming in, the two ringleaders were taken away to be beaten and then he came back and delivered a harangue which lasted all of ten minutes, made all the more effective because he brought the snivelling victims of his cane back with him. Afterwards, we were all given hefty impositions and White wasn't exempt, either. I happened to be passing the staff-room after we had been dismissed and heard Blackstone giving him the works. I can't remember the words he used, but I had never heard one adult speaking to another like that before and I was duly impressed. Unfortunately, the effects of all that didn't last and within a few weeks his classes were as rowdy as ever.

'I also remember once that Fraser, who was the school expert on anything to do with sex, asked him what adultery was. He wouldn't have dared to put a question like that to Blackstone or Hannam and Jarrett would have been able to carry it off easily, but not White; he went even paler than usual and then began to rant at Fraser, saying that he was disgusting and told him to leave the room. Fraser refused to do so and I can't think what would have ensued if the bell hadn't gone.'

'When did that happen?'

'Let me think. Yes, it must have been that last term, because Fraser was old enough to have given us a practical demonstration of his sexual maturity, if you know what I mean.'

'After my experiences with that morning cold bath routine, I know exactly what you mean. Do you think he was on to anything?'

'What exactly?'

'That there was something going on between White and Barbara Blackstone.'

Pedlow raised his eyebrows. 'I can't say that it occurred to me at the time, which is hardly surprising, really, as I hadn't got even close to the sex bit by then. Do you know what my nickname was when I first went to

Winchester? It was pinprick. Small boys can be remarkably cruel, can't they, but I must admit that they did have a point and, thinking about it now, you may have one, too. Fraser was giggling about it with one of his cronies afterwards and he must have been pretty sure of his ground with White, who would never have risked any suggestion like that being reported to Blackstone — the man was as terrified of him as the rest of us.'

'How did the boys react to Blackstone's death?'

'Excitement. I know that that must sound callous, but everyone in those days was much less neurotic about death than they are now.'

'Yes, that's perfectly true.'

'I suppose it had something to do with there having been two world wars within twenty-five years and the fact that people died so much younger in those days — I remember that we lost one boy at Brantwood from meningitis and several of the fathers and one or two elder brothers were killed in the hostilities. I didn't see Patricia at all after it happened, but I can't remember anyone else being the remotest bit upset apart from the occasion of Hannam's announcement, but I think that was more due to the drama than to any sorrow. Blackstone was a character and he certainly had charisma, but he wasn't exactly loveable, was he?'

'No, he wasn't. What do you suppose he was doing by the swimming pool in the middle of the night?'

'I didn't even know it was the middle of the night. He used to go for runs before breakfast and I seem to recall us assuming that he had slipped on the ice when doing so. It was certainly hellish cold that December — that I do remember.'

'Did you hear anything during that night?'

'To be honest, I can't remember, but I think it highly unlikely. I was the dormitory dormouse. I never heard anything at night — not even the German bombers going over. Don't you remember, you were always having to rout me out of bed in the mornings?'

We chatted on for a long time after that, but he wasn't able to tell me anything more that I didn't know already and I left by taxi at eleven, promising to send him a copy of my book if it ever came out. Who knows, I thought, perhaps one day it would. There is still nostalgia for those wartime days and they had been strange and exciting times.

10

I like to think that I have always been a decisive person, but after that evening with David Pedlow it was clear that I had either been deluding myself, or that age was catching up with me. If I had been uncertain about pursuing my enquiries before, I was doubly so now. I was quite convinced that Richard Medley hadn't been telling me the whole truth about the arsenic, but if he had been poisoning Blackstone, had he also been the one to have hit the man over the head by the swimming pool? That, on the face of it, seemed unlikely in the extreme, Medley having been such a timid small boy, but the other suspects, Hannam, Barbara Blackstone and White didn't appear to have been violent people either. As for Patricia, she hadn't been beyond laying into Fraser on a number of occasions and would certainly have had the physical strength to do it, not to mention a good enough reason after her savage beating and the very real possibility of having been subjected to sexual abuse. And suppose Henderson had been wrong about the cause of Blackstone's depressed skull fracture being due to a blow on the head rather than a fall?

In the end, curiosity triumphed over my reservations and, if nothing else, I had been promising myself a visit to a health farm for years just to find out what they were really like and it was also the case that my right shoulder had started to trouble me ever since I had gone back to playing tennis. Brantwood, though, was no ordinary health farm as far as I was concerned and I was feeling distinctly nervous that Monday morning when I stopped outside the lodge just inside the main gate. When Colin Hannam had lived in it, it had been shabby and dark, the ivy having run riot and half covering many of the windows; now, all that had been removed, the stone walls steam cleaned and harsh fluorescent lighting made the interior look clinical and antiseptic. The kitchen and front room on the ground floor had been knocked into one and it was now an office with a computer together with a small telephone exchange on the wide counter, behind which a brisk-looking young woman in a white blouse and grey suit was sitting.

'I'm Janet Cresswell,' I said, 'I made a booking on the telephone last week — you were able to fit me in as you had a cancellation and . . .'

I always talk too much when I'm nervous,

237

but for once I was able to stop when I saw that she wasn't listening, being busy tapping out something on the keyboard.

'Ah, yes. It's for five days, isn't it, Mrs Cresswell? How would you like to pay?'

'Credit card, please.'

'I'll take the details now, if I may, and you'll be able to settle any extras at the end of your stay.'

'Extras?'

'Any items from the bar in your room and drinks with your meals.'

The amount I was going to be required to pay was eye watering, but I could afford it and for once I was determined to escape from the straitjacket of my pinch-penny, puritanical forebears and damn the expense, at least that was the intention, but, being the person I am, it still made me feel distinctly uncomfortable.

'If you'd like to drive up to the house,' she said, 'our receptionist, Miss Culver, will meet you there. I hope you enjoy your stay.'

'Thank you.'

I felt even more out of my league when I parked my Astra at the rear of the house, every other car being a Mercedes, BMW or Jaguar, many of them being in the £50,000 bracket, or more. The receptionist, a woman in her mid-twenties, also in a grey suit and with her name on a card pinned to the lapel, was waiting for me there and took my case from me.

'I expect you'd like to unpack and freshen up,' she said, when she had led me round to the front of the house and up the steps into the hall. 'Perhaps you'd be good enough to come down to my office over there, say at eleven, after you've had a cup of coffee, and I'll show you round and discuss your programme with you. If you'd like to wait here for a moment, I'll get Conchita to take you to your room.'

It was a most strange experience standing in the hall while I was waiting for the chambermaid; I might even have sworn that I had never been in the place in my life before, so different was it. Instead of the creaking floorboards, there was now expensive close carpeting, the wall panelling had been sanded and polished, so that it was now honey-coloured, whereas before it had been a dingy dark brown, and a window, which previously had been bricked up, had been replaced, flooding the whole place with light.

My room was in that part of the building in which Blackstone had had his living quarters and was quite new to me. It was not unlike a standard hotel bedroom and comfortable enough with a desk, easy chair, TV, radio, tea-making equipment, fridge, telephone and an ensuite bathroom. On top of the desk, there was a folder containing details of all the facilities on offer and, something which greatly impressed me, a maroon tracksuit in the wardrobe which fitted me extremely well and no doubt partly explained why they had wanted details of my height and weight when I had made the booking.

There must have been a very large injection of capital into the place in the not too distant past, I thought, as I was being shown round by Miss Culver forty-five minutes later. The thirty-metre pool had always been a good size, but it was now completely enclosed, with a sauna, a small hydrotherapy pool and jacuzzi adjacent to it; there were also two all-weather tennis courts on what had been the games field and the gym was fully equipped with rowing machines, apparatus for lifting weights and even a treadmill with associated monitoring apparatus.

'We are getting more and more people with sports' injuries, which is Miss Blackstone's particular sphere of interest. She was a hockey international, you know, and is a member of the Sports Council.'

'I look forward to meeting her.'

'I'm afraid you won't be able to do so until Thursday; she's away until then.'

'But when I booked, I was given to

understand that she would be here.'

'Miss Blackstone is a very busy person and has been called away unexpectedly,' the woman said dismissively. 'Now, have you any particular aim in mind?'

'Yes. I've not long retired and will now have much more time to play tennis and go walking and I'd like advice on an exercise programme. My muscles are flabby and I've got a bit of trouble with my right shoulder — it catches me when I serve.'

'Any special dietary needs?'

'No, I've always eaten what comes.'

'Well, you certainly haven't got a weight problem, which is more than can be said for a lot of those who come here.'

'I was rather surprised to find that there was alcohol in the fridge in my room.'

The woman smiled. 'Miss Blackstone thinks it better to provide it rather than having guests smuggling it in. She is a great believer in people taking and being responsible for their own decisions and that's also why clients are free to choose their own diets, although we are only too happy to advise, if need be. By the way, the doctor will be available directly after lunch and will carry out a number of simple checks to make sure that you don't overdo it.'

The simple checks turned out to be

surprisingly thorough; my blood pressure was taken, my heart and lungs sounded and an electrocardiogram taken before, during and after work on the bicycle. 'No problems there,' Dr Friedmann, a young woman with a German accent, who didn't look a day older than my 19-year-old granddaughter, said, 'but don't let it go to your head, will you? Work on the apparatus will be supervised, but some people when they come here do go exercise crazy and start pulling muscles and straining tendons. I suppose they feel they have to get their money's worth.'

'I know that feeling already.'

The young doctor laughed. 'Use your stay as a primer to get yourself into a sensible routine that suits you and don't be too ambitious or expect results straight away. I think we had better defer your programme until your shoulder has been assessed properly by one of the physiotherapists. Perhaps you would report to Ursula in the gym tomorrow morning at nine o'clock wearing your tracksuit?'

If the truth be told, I was quite glad to have the opportunity to get a feel of the place before meeting Patricia and, as a start, before dinner, I wrapped up warmly and wandered round the buildings, trying to recreate the atmosphere of that winter term of 1944. Even though it was the same time of year, the contrast between the blackout of those days and the bright lights in the drive and those streaming out of the windows, let alone the alterations that had been undertaken, made that task impossible. The shed under the bathroom, on to which Tony Jarrett had climbed, had long since gone, the entrance to the gym had been restyled and the swimming pool, which had been such a feature at the side of the house, was now just part of a large and disfiguring extension.

From what the receptionist had told me and from what I had read in the brochure, Brantwood clearly didn't subscribe to the carrot juice and nut cutlet ethic and that was a considerable relief to me. Although I had no particular memory of being so, the photographs didn't lie and I was undoubtedly distinctly chubby as an adolescent and young woman, surprising, really, considering the appalling food at my boarding-school and the amount of exercise I had taken. With the passing of the years, though, I had become increasingly spare, scraggy some people would have said; however, my appetite, always healthy, had not diminished and I was looking forward to the evening meal. I was not to be disappointed. I went into the dining-room at 7.45, hesitating when I saw that every table seemed to be occupied.

'I'm afraid we're full at the moment, madam,' one of the waitresses said. 'Would you mind waiting in the lounge for a few minutes?'

'You're very welcome to join me, if you like.'

I turned and saw a very powerfully built young man, who had been sitting to my left, beginning to get up.

'Could you bear it? I'm starving.'

There was something vaguely familiar about him, which was explained immediately he introduced himself. I had seen him playing in a golf tournament on TV only a few weeks earlier and he had missed a six-foot putt for a winning birdie on the first extra hole of the play-off with an Australian, who had gone on to win at the second.

Frank had been something of a golf fanatic and although I had never played myself, I had become very interested in the game after we had retired, walking round with him more often than not and pulling his trolley. We also enjoyed going to tournaments whenever we could and watching them on TV. I was extremely glad of this because Tim Benson, although a most engaging young man with whom I was on first name terms straight away, had very little conversation apart from golf, which was an all consuming passion for him. I have one of those minds that is adept at picking up and retaining trivial and useless facts and he was clearly impressed by the fact that I knew the names of many of the players and details of some of the events.

'I enjoyed watching you winning your game against the Japanese at St Andrew's last month,' I said.

'You saw that?'

'Indeed I did. It turned the whole match.'

'Thank you. It's very different playing for a team, rather than just for oneself. The thought of letting the others down adds to the stress enormously.'

'I can well imagine that. What brings you here?'

'Pain in the forearms. I've tried everything I can think of, I've changed the size of the grips on my clubs, rested, done exercises, practised more and practised less, I've even tried all the fringe stuff, but none of it has worked.'

'And have you found the answer here?'

'I think so — thanks to Miss Blackstone.'

'I haven't met her yet.'

'A pleasure in store.'

'That was said with feeling.'

'She's one tough cookie. Ingrid, one of the more cuddly physios with a most attractive foreign accent, was doing some ergometric tests on my forearms when I first arrived, I was giving her the eye and didn't notice that madam had come in. 'If your object in coming here is to pull birds', she said, 'I'm not interested, but if you want to sort out your problem, I am. Which is it to be?''

'I see what you mean; she sounds nothing if not direct.'

'Poor Ingrid. She's one of those blondes who blush, all over as it happens, at the drop of a hat and she went absolutely scarlet.'

'That's hardly surprising.'

'Anyway, I promised to be a good boy and co-operate and after a couple of days of watching me working in the gym and swinging a club and looking at some video tapes of me on the course, she called me into her office. 'It's nothing more than muscle tension', she said. 'You're fine in practice — you've got a nice loose grip on the club — but when you're under pressure or getting angry, you clench your hands and your forearm muscles tighten. Take a look at this'. She showed me a video of me walking up the fairway in a tournament in which I lost in the play off; I was wearing short sleeves and, sure enough, my fists were clenched and you could see the muscles standing out.'

'Was that the time you missed that six-foot putt?'

Benson grinned. 'There's no hiding away, is there? In fact, she also picked up something else on the video to do with that putt. I normally take two practice swings before settling down to the putt itself and that time I took three and you could see my knuckles white on the club. I suppose I must have looked sceptical or something, because she then fished out the paper record of the EMG on my forearms — that's the recording of the muscle activity — and pointed to the area which she had marked with an arrow. 'That's what happened when I got in that dig about Ingrid yesterday', she said. The record looked as if it had gone berserk and, as Miss Blackstone explained, was showing almost maximum effort.'

'I see. What's the treatment?'

'Ingrid's showing me how to relax!' Benson rolled his eyes. 'Seriously, though, that woman Blackstone really knows about golf, which is perhaps not surprising as she plays off six herself and she's also got a great understanding of the professional game. I can remember almost exactly the words she used. 'Golf is very different from most other games in that it is so slow; you have such a lot of time in which to think about the conse-quences of making a mess of a particular shot. I have played and watched quite a bit in my time and have been interested in observing how some of the great players coped with it. Peter Thomson of Australia was my favourite — he had a way of walking down the fairway as if he owned it, positively exuding confidence, and his hands used to flap loosely as he did so — no tension there. Lee Trevino never stopped talking, to himself, his caddy, his opponent and the gallery. You will have to work out a strategy of your own. Concentrate every bit as hard as you do already on each shot, but try to shut it all out in between. Admire the view, smell the flowers, practise a foreign language; I somehow don't think you would benefit from picking out pretty girls in the gallery — we have already seen what that can do to your heart rate'. The old she-devil then fished out an ECG tracing; she might have been making it all up for all I know, but I must say, it did look pretty impressive — the wretched thing had gone haywire.'

'She's obviously quite a character, this Miss Blackstone.'

'She most certainly is and she's still mighty fit, I can tell you. I went for a run with her last week — she keeps on about how many golfers are out of condition and overweight — and I can tell you it wasn't a mere jog, either. Ingrid told me that the woman played hockey for England at one time and she did the London Marathon in about three and a half hours ten years ago.'

We passed the rest of the meal most agreeably discussing the pluses and minuses of fame and media attention and, as we got up to go, he said, 'I did enjoy talking to you. I was getting fed to the back teeth with hearing about expensive cars and share prices from the men here and about divine hairdressers and smart little restaurants from the women. I hope you weren't too bored with all that golf talk.'

'On the contrary, I found it fascinating.'

I had, too, and in particular his account of Patricia, so much so that I had no hesitation in agreeing to share a table with him again the following evening. He was a most attractive young man, not only in looks but also in personality. He was only twenty-three and it couldn't be easy, I thought, to lose one's anonymity at that age, something he was already beginning to discover. It was partly for that reason that he was finding Brantwood so relaxing; the clientele were, by and large, so preoccupied by their looks and possessions that they couldn't be bothered with a mere professional golfer, even if they had recognized him which was very doubtful and, as a result, left him alone.

Although the whole object of my visit to Brantwood had, of course, been to see Patricia, the next couple of days passed both quickly and agreeably. Ursula, also a German like Ingrid, took a look at my shoulder and started me on some Maitland's exercises, I went for a jog on the treadmill and then had a sauna and a swim. Not being used to that amount of activity, I decided to take it easy on the afternoon of the Wednesday and following a rest on my bed, I wandered around the house and grounds. My old bedroom was still there, but the large dormitories had been split up into several rooms, the big classroom was now a lounge and the old dining-room had a table tennis and pool table in it.

The wood at the far end of the old games field hadn't been cleared, though, and I found the summerhouse that Tony had told me about buried deep within it. It was a sorry sight with the wood of its walls rotting and the padlock securing the door so rusty that it fell apart when I hit it with a stone. Inside, there were still the remains of a mouldy blanket, which looked as if it had been used as a nest by the local field mice and on the floor beside it was a single hairpin.

'How have you been getting on?' Tim asked me at dinner.

'Pretty well, but I reckon I'll be as stiff as a board tomorrow.'

'Don't overdo it.'

'I won't. How about you?'

'Ingrid's been devising various ways of improving my relaxation when putting me under stress.'

'How on earth does one apply psychological stress in a gym?'

He looked round and then leaned forward across the table.

'Don't tell Miss Blackstone, but if I can get ten consecutive putts into the practice cup I brought with me, I get a reward from Ingrid. The greater distance, the greater the reward. I'm not allowed to go on and on — I have to nominate when I'm going to begin for real.'

'Did you have a good day on the greens?'

'I've had worse and I hope to do better before I leave.'

'I bet you do.'

He gave me a wicked grin and then we burst out laughing together. I'm quite sure that he would have laughed a great deal louder had he known how similar was the game I had played with Tony Jarrett in that same gym all those years ago. I very nearly did tell him, but had a strong suspicion that if I did it would get back to Ingrid, hence Ursula and quite possibly Patricia and that wouldn't have done at all.

As I had anticipated, I was extremely stiff the next morning and I asked Ursula how much exercise I should take that day.

'I'll give you a massage first and then we'll see.'

I lay on my front and she started to work on the backs of my calves and thighs and then, after a short break, on the muscles around my shoulders.

'What do you think?' I asked, when there was a brief pause.

'I think, Matron, that the years have treated you pretty well.'

I jerked my head round to see the stocky, formidable-looking woman with the ice-blue eyes and very short pepper and salt hair looking at me with a half smile on her face.

'Why not get dressed and then we can have a talk in my office?'

Although her manner was friendly enough, when I was facing her across her desk, I decided to have the first say, much as I had done with Barbara White.

'I owe you a sincere apology for not having been more open about this. You clearly know who I am, although I can't imagine how you managed to recognize me. I'd like to explain why I have come here.'

I left nothing out, nothing at all, starting

with Richard Medley's visit and finishing with my speculation about her father's death. She listened intently without asking a single question and didn't speak until I had finished.

'To get one thing straight, I didn't recognize you: the security staff told me that you seemed to be taking an unusual interest in this place, both inside and out, so they decided to have you checked out by the rather efficient debt-collecting agency that we use from time to time before I came back. We have recently had trouble with reporters from the tabloids trying to dig up stuff on some of our more newsworthy clients, which is why they are on the alert just now. They found out your maiden name and that was enough for me. Anyway, if you seriously thought that I might have been the one to kill my father, which let me say straight away I didn't, I can well understand why you decided to tread rather gingerly and get some feeling of the way I had turned out before meeting me. In your shoes, I would have done exactly the same. The one thing you haven't explained is what made you decide that I might have done such a thing.'

'The more I thought about what you told me, and the questions you no doubt remember asking me all those years ago, the more convinced did I become that your father was abusing you sexually in a particular way, not least when I discovered that he had tried the same sort of thing with Barbara. Even though I had similar suspicions at the time, quite honestly it never even occurred to me that your father died other than as the result of an accident. Recently, though, when I put the pathologist's findings, what Barbara told me and the memory of the state you were in the morning after his death, together, it seemed not unreasonable to conclude that he had tried it once too often, you had defended yourself and hit him over the head with something.'

'I see. You know, Janet, although it must have been very difficult for you to believe at the time, I was and still am very grateful to you. You were very good to me during that terrible term and if you promise not to repeat this to anyone, anyone at all, I'd like to tell you what led up to the events of that night and what had happened then and later.'

'I promise.'

'It won't make any sense unless I start at the beginning and as this may take some time I just want to make sure that there are no interruptions.'

She picked up the internal telephone and

in a few brisk sentences told her secretary that she was not on any account to be disturbed until she rang back to say that she was free.

'Right, you see . . . '

11

I only ever had the haziest memories of my mother. I could just recall being taken up to the large bedroom she shared with my father each day after tea to see the frail figure propped up against the pillows. To start with, I was allowed to climb on to the bed and my mother would read to me, but soon, even that was too much, my visits were reduced to a few minutes a couple of times a week and then stopped altogether. I was not told what had happened; my mother's name just stopped being mentioned, and it was only many years later that I discovered from my uncle that my mother had died of breast cancer in the summer of 1936, when I was only four and a half years old.

Mrs Worrall, the matron, who had effectively been looking after me for more than a year, took over completely, but that didn't last, either. In the autumn of 1938, I started as a pupil at Brantwood and from then on Mrs Worrall had less and less to do with me and, in any case, left in the summer of 1940. The arrival of her replacement, Barbara Stanhope, made little impact on me; during the term, things continued much as before and during the holidays I either went to stay with my uncle and aunt in Malvern, or went away with my father.

And what exciting trips those were! Until the outbreak of war, my father used to take me down to the Dorset coast at Lulworth, where we went camping. He taught me to pitch a tent, to make fires and to cook. I was already a strong swimmer, having learned in the pool at the school, but that was nothing compared with tackling the whole width of the cove, particularly as I had to cover the whole distance using the Australian crawl and at a good pace, which I eventually achieved. We hired a boat from one of the fishermen; I learned to row and we spent our days walking, scrambling over the rocks, fishing or rowing round to the neighbouring bays.

For me it was sheer bliss. I wore nothing but a pair of shorts or bathing trunks. I became as brown as a berry and lean, hard and fit. Even the outbreak of war didn't spoil it, despite that stretch of the Dorset coast being closed to bathing. One of the former pupils at Brantwood was the son of a farmer in the Lake District and we went up there each Easter and in the summer holidays. It was just as good as the seaside, if not better. We walked up all the peaks; I learned to climb and abseil and became expert in a canoe. Best of all was coming back in the evenings, tired and sometimes even exhausted, to a hot bath and meals of roast lamb and delicious vegetables, about which I was told to keep quiet because of the strict rationing elsewhere. Afterwards, I would snuggle up to my father and he would read to me by the light of a hurricane lamp — there was no mains electricity. It wasn't a question of soppy children's stories, either, but of stirring adventure tales by Rider Haggard and Buchan. My father's marriage to Barbara made very little difference, either. I didn't actively dislike her, but she wasn't fun like my father, spent most of her time playing the piano and the one time we did go to the Lakes on holiday together, she clearly didn't like it. She felt the cold, couldn't keep up with us on the hills and always wanted to go back whenever it started to rain. After a day or two, she hardly ventured out, spending most of her time reading in front of the open fire, and that was the last time she came on holiday with us.

Although I was unaware of it at the time, I was to think later that it was the winter of 1943 that marked the start of the change in my father. He began to beat me if I transgressed, at first using a slipper, then a hairbrush and finally the cane. I was expected to take it without complaint or a whimper, which I always managed to do, and that would elicit praise.

'That's the way, my little Spartan,' he would say. 'All is now forgiven.'

He would then ruffle my hair and it would all be forgotten until the next time. Apart from the punishments, he started to push me into attempting climbs that were at the very limit of my strength and skill, into dives from rocks which were too high for the depth of the pool below and made me canoe down rapids that were too severe. It was during our Easter holiday of the following year that the other thing began to happen as well.

The two of us had gone on the longest walk we had ever attempted with a tent and sleeping bags and in the late afternoon, the heavens had opened and we were soaked to the skin. We pitched the tent and brewed some hot soup, but even that wasn't enough to stop my uncontrollable shivering.

'Do you know what the Spartans used to do when they got thoroughly chilled like this?' my father asked me.

'No.'

'They stripped to the skin and huddled together. They didn't have sleeping bags, of course, but that makes it even better.'

It never occurred to me that there was

anything wrong, or even unusual about it as we got into one of the sleeping bags together — I had, after all, seen my father naked any number of times in the pool at school. I was colder than I had ever been in my life before and it soon began to work, too. He was right behind me and gradually the shivering began to diminish and then stopped altogether.

'When it was particularly cold,' he whispered into my ear, 'the Spartan boys used to do something else, which worked even better. You may find it unusual and perhaps feel a bit of discomfort until you get used to it, but like the Spartans, you wouldn't mind a little pain, would you?'

'All right.'

It most certainly was unusual and did hurt me, but not all that much and when he began to do other strange things with his hand, I felt a warmth building up deep inside me, a crescendo of extraordinary sensations, which culminated in a feeling almost as if I was exploding. Soon after, I fell asleep, completely relaxed and glowing. It was very cold that spring in the Lake District and my father took other opportunities to warm me up. He used some vaseline to make it easier for me and I began to look forward to the occasions when, during the night, the door of my bedroom in the farmhouse opened and he got into the narrow bed beside me.

'I think it would be best if we kept it a little secret between just the two of us, my little Spartan, don't you?' he said, just before we boarded the train on our way back to Brantwood at the end of the holiday. 'Barbara doesn't approve of you doing all the boys' things you're so good at like football, hockey and climbing and we don't want her getting into a state, do we?'

'No, Father.'

'That's the spirit.'

As I was sleeping in one of the dormitories, it didn't happen during the summer term, but when we went up to Rosthwaite again in August, the same cycle of pushing me to the very limits of my endurance and the evening visits to my bedroom began again. It was in the winter term of 1944 that I began to fear my father for the first time. His moods became more unpredictable; he began to bully the boys, particularly Medley, and after I had cheated in the exam, the beating he gave me hurt me so much that it required every ounce of my courage and self control not to cry out and beg him to stop. Even then, though, I was proud of my stoicism, knowing, as I looked at the bruises in the mirror in the bathroom, that none of the others had ever been beaten anything like as hard as that, nor would they have been able to take it like me.

Even though my father left me alone after the Ravenscourt match, the one thing I was dreading the following week was having to retake the maths test. I knew I was going to fail it and with my bottom still badly bruised and hurting even when I sat down carefully, I was just as certain that I wouldn't be able to take another caning so soon. When the morning came, I was feeling sick with anxiety as I went into Mr Hannam's classroom to find him waiting for me.

'Come and sit down, Patricia,' he said, giving me a smile.

I did so, lowering myself carefully on to the chair and looked miserably at the paper he put in front of me.

'Don't look so glum. Why don't we go over the first question together?'

It wasn't only the first one, either; for the next half-hour, Hannam sat beside me, encouraging and cajoling me and patiently explaining each step required to find the right answers.

'Well done,' he said, when at last I had finished and he opened the door for me. 'That wasn't so bad, was it?' He put his hand on my bottom and gave it a series of very gentle pats. 'Don't worry, I'll make sure your father knows how well you have done and I know how pleased he'll be.'

It wasn't easy keeping things quiet at Brantwood and it was obvious that Hannam had heard about my beating. I had always liked him; he had taken an interest in my diving and swimming, always watched what I was doing carefully and giving me helpful hints on how to improve further. I have no idea what exactly he had said to my father because the matter was never raised again and I steadily began to relax. At least I did, until I began to bleed a week or two later. I was totally ignorant about female physiology, or anatomy, for that matter, and thought that the combination of my savage beating and the tough football match had injured me internally in some way. My visit to you and our subsequent talks brought my world crashing about my ears. I had competed at games with the boys for years; I was tougher than any of them; I had revelled in all the outdoor activities with my father and thoughts of gender had never entered my head. Now, all of a sudden, the whole edifice had come tumbling down.

I desperately needed some information about what my father had been doing to me, but at the same time didn't want to give our secret away. While I was stumbling to find the right words, I saw Miss Brice's expression change and for one dreadful moment thought I had given the game away, but then the matron explained in detail 'the facts of life' and told me that what I was hinting at was a misconception and that it was something that men and women should never do together. If that was true, I thought after she had left the room, and Miss Brice seemed so confident and knowledgeable about it all, then there must be something very wrong with it. My rapidly developing body was another worry. I had suddenly become shy of it. Football had almost completely lost its attraction and I, who had never cried, whatever happened, found myself having to disappear into a quiet corner to have a weep. At that time, too, my father began to look unwell; he wasn't himself at all and didn't even watch the last football match of the season, which we won to give us an unbeaten record, even though by then my heart wasn't in it and my play a travesty of my normal form.

The night it happened, I was feeling low and irritable. I had snapped at Medley when he had offered to give me half his sticky bun when we were drinking our evening cocoa and Fraser's silly joke in the dormitory was the last straw.

'You always seem to know everything,

Pedlow,' he said. 'What's a lightning military offensive?'

'Don't you even know that, Fraser. It's a *blitzkrieg*.'

'What about a naval attack on Brest?'

'Don't be silly, there isn't a special word for that.'

'Oh yes there is. It's a *titzkrieg*.'

He started to dance around me, laughing at me and poking my tender breasts, and without conscious thought I brought my knee up and he collapsed on to the floor, ashen white, doubled up and retching. I walked straight out of the dormitory, went into the bathroom and burst into tears.

'Are you ready, Patricia?'

'Nearly, Matron.'

'Hurry up. The others are all in bed.'

I managed to get under the bedclothes without you seeing my face and for once there was no talking after lights out. I had an unpleasant ache in my stomach and tossed and turned for what seemed like hours and it seemed to me that I had only just got off to sleep, when I felt the pressure on my temple and started to sit up, only to be gently restrained. It was pitch dark behind the heavy blackout curtains, but I knew at once that it was my father from the familiar smell of garlic on his breath.

'I want you to come with me — I've got something important to tell you,' he whispered in my ear. 'Be as quiet as a mouse — we don't want to wake the others, do we?'

My dressing gown and slippers were in their usual place on top of the tuckbox at the base of my bed and I put them on, following him down the corridor, across the landing and into his study.

'I've not been feeling at all well recently, Patricia, but I'm beginning to get better, although I still can't get off to sleep. What we used to do together to get warm on holiday also helped us to sleep really well, didn't it? Do you remember?'

He smiled and took a step towards me.

'I don't want to, father. It's not right.'

'What do you mean it's not right.'

'Miss Brice said — '

'Do you know what happens to boys who can't keep secrets?'

'I'm not a boy, Father, and I didn't tell her what we did. I just asked her . . . '

He took hold of me roughly and pulled off my dressing-gown.

'You will now take off your pyjama trousers, bend over that chair and then we'll see what happens to boys who disobey me.'

I saw him reach for the cane which was resting against the wall and made a dash for the door. Without thinking, I went down the stairs two at a time and tried to get out of the front door, but it was both locked and bolted and I was still struggling with it, when I saw the dark shape of my father already halfway down to the hall and I wrenched open the door of the small cloakroom to my right and slammed it behind me. The bolt on it was only a flimsy affair and directly he put his shoulder to it, I heard it begin to give. I pulled the curtain across, opened the small window, somehow managed to squeeze through it and jumped down, landing on a flower bed.

I picked myself up and sprinted across the drive towards the protection of the trees and just short of them was glancing back when I tripped over the verge and measured my length on the grass, knocking all the breath out of my body. I heard the loud creak as the front door came open only twenty yards from me and then my father's hoarse whisper.

'Patricia! Patricia!'

I lay there motionless, desperately trying to control my breathing, and a minute or two later, turned my head cautiously and looked back. It was very dark and although I was able to make out the outline of the building, there was no sign of my father and I crawled towards one of the trees and stood up behind it. I shrank back when I saw the wavering light from a torch at the front door and when it disappeared round the side of the house, I stood there for a moment in an agony of indecision when a hand was suddenly clamped over my mouth.

'It's all right, Patricia, it's only me — Colin Hannam. Listen, I saw what happened. You can't stay here, you'll freeze to death, so why not go down to the Lodge? There's a good fire in the living-room and I'll join you when I've had a word with your father. Don't worry, I'll be able to calm him down and everything will be all right, I know it will, and I won't let him beat you again, I promise.'

I gave a shudder of disgust as he pressed against me and kissed me on the lips. I had changed completely since I had started my period and had had those chats with Miss Brice. No longer did the way Hannam used to look at me seem just friendly when, naked on the diving board, I was being shown by him how to do a handstand before somer-saulting into the water. I also hadn't liked the way he had helped me on with my Robin Hood costume, or made Watson undress completely in front of him in the Lodge.

No, I wasn't going to go down there and, my mind made up, I waited until he strode off in the direction of the flickering light and then slipped across the drive and in through the now open front door and up the stairs. At the top, I hesitated for a moment. Had I made the right decision? It really was perishing cold outside and I couldn't possibly have stayed out in the open all night, but would Mr Hannam succeed in calming my father down, or would he refuse to listen and realize that I had come back in? And what would he do to me if he found me?

There was one place which I knew had a lock on the door and that was the bathroom I shared with you. Even if my father discovered that I was in there, the matron's bedroom was right opposite and she would be certain to come to investigate if he tried to break in and I screamed. I locked myself in, put the back of the chair under the handle of the door and was still there hours later, shivering with cold, when I heard the soft knock on the door.

'Are you in there, Patricia? You won't be long, will you? Patricia, are you all right?'

I hardly took in what you were saying either then, or later, and after I had been taken to the sickbay, I was lying on the bed in a daze when the door opened and I gave a violent start when I saw that it was my stepmother.

'Patricia, your father's had a bad accident.'

I sat up and looked straight at the woman

who failed to meet my gaze.

'He's dead, isn't he?'

'I'm afraid so.'

The woman held out her arms, but I slipped out of bed, ducked under them and ran down the stairs and out into the grounds. When I was out of breath and exhausted, I crept into the gym and curled up on one of the benches, rocking backwards and forwards and moaning in my distress. All that had happened in the preceding two months had been more than enough for me and now, the man whom I had worshipped, loved more than anyone else in the world and finally come to fear, was dead and hadn't I been partly responsible for that, too?

I had no idea how long I remained there, only that some time, a long time later, you arrived and without saying anything, sat down beside me, taking me gently in your arms until at last I calmed down. For the rest of that day, I'm sure you remember that you hardly left me for more than a few minutes. You brought me tempting snacks; you protected me from people, including my stepmother whom I didn't want to see; you made up the other bed in the sickbay so that I wouldn't have to sleep alone and, above all, you talked to me. You seemed to understand how much I had loved my father and encouraged me to speak about him, particularly the good times we had had together and what a wonderful man he had been.

I never did have to face my stepmother or the boys; my uncle arrived from Malvern, you helped me to pack some clothes and my few treasures and then I went off with him in the train. My uncle Gerald was a solicitor, a lot older than my father, and although I had spent part of one or two of the school holidays with them, my father had usually been there, too, and I had never got to know him, or Aunt Elaine, all that well.

I was to think later that the two of them had had endless patience with me and they needed every ounce of it. Neither of them was young — they had two grown-up sons in the forces — and it couldn't have been easy for them to have a truculent, aggressive girl of nearly thirteen descending on them. They did their best to make Christmas a happy time for me with a party and a visit to the local pantomime, but throughout it I remained sullen and uncommunicative.

'I've managed to get you a place at the Malvern College for Girls in September,' my uncle said to me one day in early March, when I had almost completed my first term in a small private school up the road from where they lived.

'I don't want to go there.'

'We all have to do some things we don't like. You'll just have to make the best of it and if you do that, you'll find yourself enjoying it — it's one of the best schools for girls in the country.'

'You're only sending me there to get rid of me.'

'If that were true, Patricia, we would have sent you to a boarding-school somewhere on the other side of the country, not as a day girl only up the road.'

'I hate you.'

'You have no reason to hate either of us, and if you go on like this you are going to become and remain unhappy, very unhappy indeed.'

'Why don't you beat me? My father used to when I was bad.'

'Beating people is not the way to make them happy, or to get them to behave. One of these days I hope you'll understand that.'

I flung out of the room, knowing that I was being horrid and unreasonable and hating myself for it. If I couldn't get any reaction out of my uncle and aunt and they weren't going to punish me, then I would have to punish myself. I waited until they were out, then stripped off all my clothes, took hold of my uncle's razor strop from the bathroom and beat myself in front of the full-length mirror in their bedroom until the whole of my back was covered in angry welts.

That was the turning point; I was both deeply ashamed of what I had done to myself and, even more, of the way I had been behaving to my uncle and aunt. After supper that evening, I went up to my room, waited for several minutes, then went back down the stairs and paused outside the sitting-room door, gritting my teeth and trying desperately to pluck up enough courage to go in. All of a sudden, in a series of rapid movements, I threw the door open and once inside, stood with my back to it and, trying unsuccessfully to keep my voice steady, said, 'I've come to say I'm sorry. I've not been nice to you at all and I'm really sorry, I . . . '

Feeling the tears about to come and with my cheeks blazing, I fled back to my room and took refuge under the bedclothes. There was a gentle knock on the door half an hour or so later and then my aunt came in to sit on the side of the bed without turning on the light.

'Your uncle and I both think that that was very brave of you, Patricia. I won't say any more now, but we both love you very much and we're going to have such fun together, I just know we are.'

She bent forward, kissed me on the cheek, then walked quietly out of the room. Not everything fell into place straight away, but I began to talk to them, then to chatter, particularly to my aunt, and the final breakthrough with my uncle came on my thirteenth birthday at the end of March. It was a Saturday and not only did he take me into the town in the morning to select a new hockey stick, but that afternoon we went to watch the girls' college first eleven playing in a match. I was enthralled; the players were so quick, their stick-work brilliant and they hit the ball so hard.

'One day, Uncle Gerald,' I said at the end of the game, 'I'm going to be every bit as good as they are.'

'If you work hard at it, I'm quite sure you will be.'

After that, there was no question of my not wanting to go to the college, in fact I couldn't wait to do so. My days there were happy ones. The tight discipline suited me well and although academically it was a bit of a struggle, I did manage to get some of the new O levels with a lot of help from my uncle at home, and the games were a delight. I turned out to be the best all-rounder the school had ever had, excelling at cricket, swimming and gymnastics, but it was at hockey that I really made my mark. Captain of the eleven, I was selected to play for England two years after I left when I was training to be a physiotherapist at St Thomas's Hospital.

Just before I went up to London, I took my uncle and aunt out to dinner as a thank you present and afterwards, gave him a leather wallet and her a handbag. Afterwards, when they got home, my uncle gave me a kiss.

'That was a splendid evening,' he said. 'It was a really kind thought and the presents are quite lovely. We are both very proud of you and wish you every success in the future.'

It could have sounded forced and pompous, but it didn't — I understood that he really meant it and on my side, I owed him so much. As for my aunt, she was the mother I had never had. She was fun, but she was also warm and cuddly and we had endless chats and discussions about everything under the sun. She was also the most wonderful recipient of presents, obviously getting enormous pleasure out of them; not only was she good at saying thank you, but, as with the handbag, she continued to demonstrate her appreciation for weeks afterwards by giving me little glances and gestures whenever she was carrying it.

Before taking me to the station on my way to London, my uncle took me into his study.

'Before you leave us, Pat, there are one or two things I'd like to discuss with you. I know that latterly there were occasions when your father was cruel to you, but he wasn't well for some time before his accident and I only discovered exactly what was wrong with him after his death. I am quite convinced that his illness, and in particular the brain tumour he had, explains all his uncertain and unnatural behaviour of which you were the victim and I wouldn't want you to judge him too harshly.'

He went on to explain all about the tuberous sclerosis.

'Looking back, I think it possible that my mother, your grandmother, might also have had the same condition. She certainly had turns which could have been epilepsy, but it wasn't something that was ever discussed at the time. Although it's very unlikely that you are affected, why not have a talk with a neurologist? Have a think about it and if it strikes you as a good idea, I'd be glad to fix it up.'

My uncle certainly knew how to handle me, I was to think later. If he had told me to see someone, I am almost sure that I would have refused, but having planted the seed, he left it at that and shortly afterwards I went to Harley Street for a consultation. The man listened to the history carefully, gave me a

276

meticulous examination and then explained the situation clearly and directly.

'You have absolutely no sign of the condition at present,' he said, 'and I think it highly unlikely that you will develop it, but there is, unfortunately, no way of being one hundred per cent certain. Why not come again later should you be worried about it in any way or, in view of the hereditary factors, which we have already discussed, should you be contemplating marriage and a family, I would be only too pleased to take another look at you. Who knows, by then there may be better tests available. There is an investigation called air encephalography, which could be carried out now, but it is both unpleasant and is associated with a certain amount of risk and I wouldn't recommend you to have it at present.'

★ ★ ★

'I never did go back to see the neurologist, largely because marriage was never seriously on my agenda. The sex thing has never worked, or perhaps it would be more accurate to say that I didn't allow it to. I very soon discovered that it wasn't possible to practise the sado-masochistic games that turned me on without meeting men who were even more disturbed than I was, and dangerous, too. After one near disastrous relationship with an older man, it seemed best to put that side of life to one side. Would it have been different had it not been for my father and his illness? Probably, but I have never been one to dwell on imponderables. I have made many good friends of both sexes both on and off the sports field and although there have been times when I would have liked children and family life, I know perfectly well that neither would have suited me.'

'You know, Patricia, from what you said at the time, I suspected what your father had been doing to you and I find it difficult to forgive myself for not having intervened.'

'I'm very glad that you didn't. After all, it had all happened by then, and if you had reported it, the consequences would have been disastrous. Just think, if the authorities had believed it, poor old Dad might have finished up in prison and if they didn't, I shudder to think what he would have done to me. As it turned out, I had the great good fortune to be looked after by the most wonderful adoptive parents you could imagine and I'm still very much part of the family, getting on well with both my cousins, their wives and children. I'm a godmother twice over and that gives me a lot of pleasure and fulfilment, too.'

'You've certainly made a great success of this place; how on earth did you manage to get it off the ground?'

'Through my cousin Jack, who was pretty big in the City before he retired. I rented it to a commune for a time in the sixties and seventies, but when that folded I had the idea of going into the health-farm business and he supported me enthusiastically, raising most of the money and helping me to set up the company of which he is one of the directors. I suppose we were lucky in that we hit the right time just when people were beginning to get into diets, health foods and exercise, but you can't stand still in this business and fairly recently I decided to move more in the direction of sports' medicine. Games players and athletes are some of the really big money earners at present and the medical facilities for them have started to take off in a big way. Before unification, East Germany used to be easily the best place for it and that's where I picked up a lot of ideas, needless to say, though, without the performance-enhancing drugs, which were the downside of their activities. In addition, I recruited many of the staff from people who were done out of a job when the state subsidies ceased to be available. I have also formed a mobile unit, which goes to various sporting events and is also largely staffed by them.'

'Hence Ursula, Ingrid and Dr Friedmann?'

'Exactly.'

'The pathologist I talked to seems quite certain that your father was both being poisoned with arsenic and died by drowning, having fallen into the pool after having been hit on the head by some sort of blunt instrument. If he's right, who do you think might have done it?'

'Looking back, I think I always suspected that Colin Hannam had been responsible for my father's death. It was very fortunate for me that I was able to discuss it with my uncle when he judged that I was mature enough to be told about the man's suicide and the fact that my father had changed his will. Thanks also to my uncle's wisdom and knowledge of human nature, I was much less troubled by the whole business, including Hannam's paedophile tendencies, than I would have been otherwise. As to poisoning with arsenic, all I can tell you is that it had nothing to do with me.'

'Do you remember if Hannam was carrying anything when he left you that night?'

'Come to think of it, he did have a heavy walking stick with him. Not only did I feel it when he put his arms around me, but I also saw him using it when he strode off towards the pool. You know, Janet, your visit here has not only given me the opportunity to talk about the whole thing properly really for the first time, but also the chance to say a sincere thank you for all the kindness and very real help you gave me during that term.'

'It's very nice of you to say that and for my part, it's a great relief to find that you managed to cope with the whole thing so well and to have put together such a thriving business now. I take it that you don't wish to see Richard Medley.'

'I most certainly do not. As far as I am concerned it is time to draw a firm and final line under the whole affair. Medley and I helped each other in a number of ways when we were here together and I can understand his thinking very clearly, but as far as I am concerned, I have no intention of meeting him now, or at any time in the future. Reliving those days and meeting some of the people involved has obviously helped you to get over your bereavement, but you were an adult at the time and on the outside looking in and, in any case, our talk today is as much introspection as I am prepared to go in for. I would also like you to tell Richard Medley that should he try to make an approach he will be rebuffed and that goes for everyone else you have met including Barbara, although I can't imagine that she would want to see me again.' Patricia Blackstone gave me the suspicion of a smile. 'I don't expect that you would put it quite like that — I'm quite sure that you're a much more tactful person than I am — but no doubt you'll be able to get the message across. You can also tell Medley that I loved my father, that his illness explains much of his behaviour towards the two of us. I forgive him and I hope that he does, too. Now, I think that's quite enough soul-searching for one day, don't you? According to Ursula, you need some more treatment for that shoulder and you'll be in good hands with her. Now, I'll say goodbye — we won't be seeing each other again. And . . . Janet!'

'Yes, Patricia?'

'People in my employment gossip about me at their peril; in fact, not to put too fine a point on it, they make a rapid exit. Now Ursula is an excellent worker and a nice girl, but she is not English; she is not very sophisticated and I would not like to lose her. I trust I make myself clear.'

'As crystal.'

'Good.'

The woman smiled, gave me a brisk

handshake and then rang for her secretary to show me out.

★ ★ ★

I left Patricia Blackstone's office feeling more than a bit shell-shocked. I liked what I had seen of her — I have always admired people who are direct and say exactly what they mean, partly because I am so bad at that myself — but she was still every bit as tough as she had been all those years ago and ruthless, too, I wouldn't have minded betting. I had seen the way her secretary had looked at her when she had come in to show me out and there was also what she had said just before I left the room. As well as being tough, she had also disconcertingly read me like a book. I had been intending to find out a bit more about her from Ursula and Ingrid, too, for that matter, but she had neatly put the stoppers on that. I was certainly not going to be responsible for jeopardizing the jobs of those young women.

With the pressure off, I thoroughly enjoyed the final two days of my stay; my shoulder improved out of all recognition and even without being able to serve properly, I was more than a match for Tim at both tennis and table tennis and, for good measure, he gave

283

me some golf lessons.

'What a pity you didn't take it up years ago,' he said just before I left. 'You would have been really good. Why not start now?'

'I'm far too old.'

'Nonsense. I've known several people of over eighty who've been able to beat their age and you could easily be another in a few years' time.'

He took my address, promising to send me a couple of tickets for next year's Open Championship, and although I had had offers like that before from patients and nothing had come of them, I had an instinct that he really meant it. I liked Tim Benson immensely and I think he liked me.

12

I needed a little time to digest all that I had learned, at least that is what I told myself, but in reality what I was doing was trying to pluck up enough courage to have another talk with Richard Medley. After another couple of days, though, I gave myself a brisk talking to and wrote him a brief note inviting him for tea on the following Sunday before my resolution failed completely. Fortunately for me, I badly underestimated both the efficiency of the post office and the speed with which Richard Medley might respond, because his call came through only two days later. Predictably, too, he arrived on the dot of four that Sunday afternoon.

'I'm sorry it's taken me so long,' I said, when I had settled him in one of the armchairs on the opposite side of the fireplace to where I was sitting and had given him a cup of tea and a slice of chocolate cake, 'but it proved a much more complicated task than I had expected.'

'I don't understand. I thought you were just going to Brantwood to sound out Patricia about meeting me.'

'That was my original intention, but before doing so, I began to dig deeply into my memories of that term and, as a result, began to look into the circumstances of Blackstone's death. It wasn't an accident, Richard; someone hit him over the head and that's why he fell into the swimming pool and drowned — I have no doubt about that at all. It must have happened round about midnight, because long enough time had gone by for the ice to have formed over him by the time he was found by Stacey. Not only that, he was being poisoned by arsenic. How can I be so sure? It is because Blackstone suffered from a condition called tuberous sclerosis; he was a patient at the London Neurological Centre and he left his body to them for research purposes. They had kept some specimens from the post-mortem examination, one of which was of his left foot to show the presence of a small fibroma under his big toenail, and arsenic was present from a paring from one of the others. One other thing was quite clear from a sketch made of the vertex of his skull that there was a depressed fracture at that site, which the pathologist is convinced could not have been caused by a fall and must have been due to a blow with a blunt instrument.'

'That all sounds very far fetched to me.

Blackstone was always taking pills of one sort or another and he was probably using arsenic as a tonic — people did in those days.'

'In Victorian times, perhaps, but not in 1944. Blackstone wasn't at all well towards the end of that term; he was off his food and had very dry and scaly skin. The neurologist who was treating his epilepsy thought it was due to bromide intoxication, but the man himself was convinced that his wife, Barbara, was poisoning him. He was being poisoned all right, but having seen her recently, I don't think she was responsible.' I suddenly looked up at him. 'I think you were, Richard.'

The man blinked at me behind his glasses. 'And what leads you to that extraordinary conclusion?'

'You no doubt remember telling me about the bottle of arsenic in Hannam's classroom and how tempted you were to poison Blackstone with it. I was struck at the time by the amount of detail you went into, even quoting the case of Madeleine Smith. I have since talked to one of the other boys who was in your form: there wasn't a bottle of arsenic in that room, was there Richard? I gather that you liked to read about famous murder trials and no doubt the case of Madeleine Smith featured in one of the books, but the theory of her having painted an intimate part of her

287

body with arsenic paste and getting her lover to lick it off wasn't put forward until a new book was written in the seventies. I think you must have read that book fairly recently and I don't believe that it's a coincidence that you suggested just now that Blackstone might have taken the arsenic as a tonic — exactly the same thing was said about Madeleine Smith's lover.

'Why did you describe that incident to me in such graphic detail? Was it your way of dropping a hint to me that you were ready to admit it, or were you trying to put the blame on Hannam? I did consider the possibility that he was responsible, but at the time the poisoning started, he had no reason to want to harm Blackstone. In fact, the very reverse was true; that school was his one haven after he had been devastated by his First World War experiences.'

'You said that Blackstone thought that his wife was poisoning him — he must have had some reason for thinking that.'

'He was becoming paranoid as the result of tuberous sclerosis, which was affecting the fronto-temporal lobes of his brain and also explained other facets of his behaviour, but he became convinced that she wasn't the culprit after he had laid on a demonstration that he asked me to witness.'

I explained how Blackstone had made Barbara drink the hot chocolate after his meal one evening and all the time, Medley stared at me from behind his thick glasses.

'And what about the man's fall into the swimming pool? I suppose you think I was responsible for that, too.'

'No, as it happens, I don't. The night he died, Patricia told me that her father came into the dormitory to fetch her. He had been sexually abusing her for some time and although he had stopped doing so at the end of the summer holidays, after he began to recover from his illness, the compulsion must have got to him again. Patricia, though, had changed a great deal during the course of that term. She had started her periods, as a result had had a few chats with me and although she didn't tell me exactly what her father had been doing to her, I had a shrewd idea from her strange ideas about how sexual inter-course took place and, without being too specific about it, I made her realize that activities such as those she had hinted at were both wrong and unnatural. As a result, she refused to co-operate with him that night and when it became clear that he was proposing to beat her until she changed her mind, she ran off down the main staircase.

'She bolted herself into the downstairs

cloakroom as she was unable to open the front door of the building and when her father tried to force his way in, she climbed out of the window. The opening was too small for him to follow and while he was unbolting and unlocking the front door and looking for a torch, she ran across the lawn and into the trees. Colin Hannam, who suffered from terrible nightmares as the result of his wartime experiences, was in the habit of walking round the grounds at night, must have seen what was happening and when Blackstone came out of the house, he told Patricia to go to the Lodge and that he would calm her father down. It's quite impossible now to know the exact sequence of events, but, for whatever reason, I believe that Hannam must have hit Blackstone on the head with the knob at the end of his stick, and he then fell, unconscious, into the pool and drowned.

'Patricia didn't go to the Lodge because, for the reasons I just mentioned, she had become more sexually aware and knew that Hannam was also interested in her in that way. She locked herself in the bathroom which she and I shared and that's where I found her the following morning.'

'And you believed what she told you?'

'Oh yes.'

'I see. And what happened to Hannam?'

'You've already told me how much you liked him so I know that you'll be sorry to hear that he shot himself on Christmas day only a few weeks after the school closed.'

Medley shook his head. 'Is Patricia prepared to see me?'

'No, she isn't, and she was extremely clear about it. If you value my advice, you won't try to persuade her to change her mind; I'm quite sure that you wouldn't succeed and I also think that it would only add to her and your unhappiness. Patricia has made a great success of her life by determinedly looking forward rather than back and she's not about to change tack now. She also asked me to tell you that she was convinced that her father's behaviour towards her latterly was the result of the abnormalities in his brain due to his illness, that she forgave him and hoped that you would, too.'

'She said that?' I nodded. 'And she seemed quite happy?'

'Yes, I have no doubt of that at all.'

'I'm glad about that.' There was a very long pause and then Medley suddenly looked up. 'I can't pretend to understand how you have been able to get so close to the mark after all this time, but I would like to tell you exactly what happened as far as I was concerned.'

It was on the Sunday, the day after the Brantwood match, that I finally decided that I was going to have to find a way of stopping Blackstone. If I didn't, something terrible was going to happen either to Patricia or myself and very soon at that — I was quite certain of it. She had told me only that morning that she was to be set a special maths test and that her father had said if she didn't pass it, she knew what to expect. I was willing to coach her, for hours if need be, but she only had a little over two weeks in which to prepare for it and I knew that the whole term wouldn't be long enough. Poor Patricia just didn't seem able to take in the most simple of mathematical concepts and if she were to be beaten again, surely even she wouldn't be able to take it. And if she really were to break down, I realized, young as I was, that it would destroy something in her for ever.

My favourite character in the book on famous trials, which I had read and re-read endless times, was Madeleine Smith. Not only did it seem near certain that she had poisoned her lover with arsenic, but she had got away with it and lived a long and seemingly not unhappy life. If it had worked for her, why shouldn't I try the same thing?

There was even a bottle of arsenic solution in Stacey's shed near the greenhouse. I had seen it on a shelf in there when Blackstone had sent me to fetch a fork so that he could spike the football pitch, which hadn't drained properly after a downpour. It had a large and impressive label on it with POISON in large red letters printed on the top of it and underneath: *Concentrated arsenic. To use as weed killer, dilute with twenty parts of water to one of the solution. Keep well away from children and pets.*

It seemed likely that Madeleine Smith had put arsenic powder into cups of either hot chocolate or cocoa, but that wouldn't be any good in Blackstone's case; there was no possibility of tampering with his hot drinks. It was when I was reading about the properties of arsenic in the large textbook of chemistry in Hannam's classroom that a sentence at the end of the section caught my eye and it gave me the idea of how I might do it: *If taken over a period of time, arsenic may produce a garlic-like odour on the breath.* Blackstone was always eating garlic — he had a special bowl containing the powder in the cupboard in the dining-room and was in the habit of sprinkling some over his main course at every lunchtime. He also smelled of the stuff and so no one would notice anything extra on his breath.

I was a careful and obsessional boy and wasn't going to do anything in too much of a hurry, remembering what Hannam had said to us once. 'It is important to understand scientific method. A theory is proposed, experiments are devised to put it to the test and only when those experiments have confirmed its validity are the results put to practical use'. The first essential was to get the materials for my experiment and that, I knew, would be the most dangerous part.

Taking a suitable bottle from the sickbay was simple. I heard Miss Brice splashing in the bath — I was quite certain that it was her, because Patricia, the only other person to use it, was playing table tennis in the gym — so I nipped in and removed an almost empty bottle of syrup of figs. Getting hold of the garlic and arsenic, though, was a different matter and I died many deaths before I was back in the classroom with both of them. There was the worry that I might have been seen, that I might not be able to get into the shed, or that Stacey might have used up all the weed killer. Luck, though, was with me. I nearly lost my nerve when I heard Mrs Stacey moving about in the kitchen next to the dining-room, but it was the work of only a few seconds to scoop up some of the garlic in an envelope and everything also went well in the shed. Stacey had padlocked the door, but one of the windows at the side hadn't been closed properly and I was able to open it and climb through.

I suppose I ought to have anticipated it from reading Madeleine Smith's story, but I hadn't and my frustration at finding the arsenic solution had had artificial colouring added to it was intense. Besides that, when I mixed a drop or two with the garlic on a filter paper, the powder immediately coalesced into sizeable lumps. I was deeply disappointed, but I was not going to give up and after throwing the garlic away, I hid the bottle containing the arsenic in one of the lavatory cisterns in the communal washroom near the gym. Surely, I thought, there must be some other way of doing it.

The idea came to me the very next day. On Mondays, we always had shepherd's pie made from the Sunday roast and, as I saw Blackstone vigorously shaking the bottle of Worcestershire sauce over it, I realized at once that it would be the ideal medium for disguising both the taste of the arsenic and its colour which would be hidden by the brown liquid and, most importantly of all, the headmaster consumed large quantities of it. He used it on whatever he was eating, meat, fish or sausages and he even shook it into the tomato juice he liked to have with his breakfast. What could be better, particularly as the bottle was for his exclusive use? I managed to remove the sauce bottle after games that afternoon and back in the classroom mixed the two liquids in a test tube and shook it hard. It was perfect; nothing precipitated out, the colour difference was hardly detectable and the smell of the sauce seemed unchanged. I had taken a good deal of the arsenic solution from the shed and after I had concentrated it even further by boiling it in a beaker over a Bunsen burner, put a sizeable quantity into the sauce bottle. Curiously enough, removing and replacing the tight stopper without cracking the glass proved to be the trickiest part of the whole exercise, but I achieved it in the end.

After that, all I had to do was put the sauce bottle back in the dining-room, which I achieved without incident. I could have shouted out loud in triumph a week later. It was working, it really was. First of all, Blackstone began to lose his appetite, although he still continued to drink the tomato juice in larger quantities than usual as he seemed very thirsty. He doubled up after breakfast one day and, after he had hurried out, I heard him retching in the lavatory along the corridor. He also looked unwell, his skin was dry and scaly and, best of all, the man left me and Patricia alone. As far as the maths test was concerned, she told me that it had gone quite well, which I found difficult to believe, but certainly there were no repercussions following it.

I never did discover what happened to that bottle of sauce. Had Blackstone finished it, had it been broken, had the man gone off the taste, or had he even suspected something? Whatever the reason, one morning it had disappeared. It was not replaced and slowly but surely Blackstone began to improve. A lot of his snap came back, but at least, I thought, the illness that I had provoked had bought both Patricia and me time and there were only two weeks of the term to run.

I had always been a light sleeper and the war had made it worse. The others seemed to be able to ignore the pulsing of the German bombers in the night sky, but I couldn't. Throughout the war, not a single bomb fell near the school and yet, in my imagination, I began to hear the whistle of their descent and saw myself mutilated and torn by the blast. It was as bad, if not worse, with the flying bombs — I was always waiting for the engines to cut out — and it got so bad that the slightest noise would wake me. The night it happened, the click that the door gave as it came open had me instantly alert. At first, I wasn't sure what it was that had disturbed me, but then there was a creak of a floorboard and I felt rather than saw the figure as it eased between my bed and Patricia's. Even before I heard the whispered voice, I knew that it was Blackstone; the familiar smell of pipe tobacco, which permeated his clothes, came through to me quite clearly.

'I want you to come with me . . . '

I was just able to make out those few words, then the rest was lost in the rustle of bedclothes as Patricia sat up. When I heard the door close behind them, I got out of bed, put on my slippers and dressing-gown and, taking care not to make any noise, went outside and along the corridor. I could see light coming from beneath the door of Blackstone's study and, hearing the mutter of voices from inside, walked towards it, slipping into the sickbay, which was the last room on the corridor before the landing. I was only half inside when the door of the study suddenly burst open and Patricia went flying down the stairs, taking them two at a time, to be followed moments later by her father.

Ever since, I have been deeply ashamed of

what happened next. I did none of the things I was to imagine and relive during my adolescence and even later on. Robin Hood and Errol Flynn were very much in my mind at that time and in my imagination I had fought a duel with Blackstone on the surround of the swimming pool, finally dispatched him with a thrust from my rapier and rescued Patricia, who had been tied to the bars in the gym and was about to be whipped. The truth, of course, was quite different. I slunk back to my bed and tried to pretend either that I had imagined the whole thing or that it had been a dream.

★   ★   ★

Richard Medley let out a deep sigh. 'In time, I did manage to forget about it all, but it really was the case that looking through my mother's scrapbook brought it all back. I'm not a complete idiot and knew perfectly well at an intellectual level that Patricia would be highly unlikely to want either to see me again or have old traumas raked up, but it was my wretched obsessional personality that wouldn't allow me to let it go. It may sound ridiculous now, but at the time I really loved that girl and I mean that in every sense of the word. She was so strong, brave and honest and was always coming to my rescue. Even though I was too young and ignorant to recognize it, there was an undoubted sex element as well. It had started in the gym when I felt the warm skin of her back under my fingers as I jumped over her and when we had kissed each other. Then, when I saw an even more intimate glimpse of her when she showed us her bruised bottom in the dormitory, I was not only horrified at what her father had done to her, but I was also excited — hence, no doubt, my later fantasies.

'Thanks to you, Janet, although it must sound like a sudden and unconvincing conversion, I really believe that at long last I will be able to put it all out of my mind. If I were to see her now, it would no doubt spoil my happy memories of her and, from what you've said, she clearly feels the same way about me.

'The one thing I'm really sorry about, though, is poor Hannam. Over the years, I have read a lot about the First World War and it clearly destroyed him. He was so kind to me and taught me so much, not least a fascination with the game of chess. Incidentally, you were quite right about that Madeleine Smith arsenic story that I claimed that Hannam had told us — it was yet another example of my improving on stories. I suppose I do it to show myself and events in a dramatic light — pathetic, isn't it? It's no doubt going to embarrass you, but it wasn't only Patricia that brought me down here. I also wanted to see you again and believe me, it hasn't been a disappointment, either. You're still the confident cheerful person who was so kind to me all those years ago and I'm deeply grateful for what you did for me then and have done so again now.'

★ ★ ★

The next few days were a distinct anticlimax, leaving me feeling flat and let down after all the activity and excitement then I received another letter from Richard Medley.

Dear Janet
Renewed thanks for all your effort on my behalf. I have been lucky enough to get hold of tickets for Lucia di Lammermoor at the Royal Opera House on Thursday week. In the unlikely event of your feeling robust enough to come both to it and to dinner beforehand, be assured that the words Brantwood and Blackstone won't cross my lips, nor will I drone on

about 'the slings and arrows of outra-
geous fortune', which I now see have not
rained down on my head anything like so
hard as I previously believed.
With my very best wishes
Richard

Had the man really got a sense of humour
hidden under that sensitive skin of his? I
wasn't sure, but it would be fun trying to
find out. How extraordinary, I thought, that
it should have taken me all those years to
discover that it was perfectly possible for me
to have interesting conversation and enjoy
the company of men with neither tension
nor sexual overtones. It had happened with
Alastair Henderson and David Pedlow, so
why not with Richard Medley, too, funny
old stick though he was? I was smiling to
myself as I composed my acceptance to his
invitation.

★   ★   ★

I sat for a long time with my eyes closed
after I had finished reading the manuscript,
remembering the conscientious family doctor,
the kindly, reliable and loving mother and
grandmother, but I now realized that there
had been so much more to her than that and

I felt even greater relief that she had been spared a long, diminishing and humiliating end. I stood up, recharged my glass and raised it a fraction.

'Good for you, Ma,' I said aloud. 'Good for you!'

We do hope that you have enjoyed reading this large print book.

Did you know that all of our titles are available for purchase?

We publish a wide range of high quality large print books including:
Romances, Mysteries, Classics
General Fiction
Non Fiction and Westerns

Special interest titles available in large print are:
The Little Oxford Dictionary
Music Book
Song Book
Hymn Book
Service Book

Also available from us courtesy of Oxford University Press:
Young Readers' Dictionary
(large print edition)
Young Readers' Thesaurus
(large print edition)

For further information or a free brochure, please contact us at:
Ulverscroft Large Print Books Ltd.,
The Green, Bradgate Road, Anstey,
Leicester, LE7 7FU, England.
Tel: (00 44) 0116 236 4325
Fax: (00 44) 0116 234 0205

LOCKED IN

Peter Conway

Is Father Carey a saint or sinner? Comforter of the sick — or a heavy drinker not to be trusted with secrets, confessional or otherwise? Opinion at St Cuthbert's Hospital is divided. Michael Donovan, paralysed after a rugby accident, views him as the only person to give him support. But when Father Carey is poisoned, Donovan loses the will to live. On a respirator and locked inside his paralysed body there is nothing he can do about it. Or is there? Though unable to speak or move, there is nothing inactive about his mind. Can he find a way to track down the killer?

WITH A NARROW BLADE

Faith Martin

When an elderly lady is stabbed to death in her own home, DI Hillary Greene is instantly puzzled. There's no appearance of a robbery; Flo Jenkins, popular with her neighbours, hadn't an enemy in the world. And everyone knew that, riddled with cancer, she'd only weeks left to live. Why kill a dying woman? Greene's investigation is not helped when her new DC turns out to have a violent temper and an uncertain past. With no forensics, no leads and only a junkie grandson as a suspect, is this going to be Hillary Greene's first failure on a murder case?